"What Could This Be?" Jefferson Murmured.

The last envelope bore a name. His name, written in a hand he knew. For one stunned moment Jefferson thought it was a cruel hoax. When he drew out two sheets of paper, he knew it wasn't. The first was newspaper. The second a plain white sheet torn raggedly from a tablet. One line was written across the sheet in the same familiar hand.

Catching an unsteady breath, Jefferson read the written words out loud. His own words, spoken just once, long ago.

If you ever need me...

A promise to keep. A promise only Marissa would know.

"I'll come for you," he finished.

Marissa was alive. Given the subterfuge of the message, she was in danger. She needed help. She needed Jefferson Cade.

Dear Reader,

Ring in the New Year with the hottest new love stories from Silhouette Desire! *The Redemption of Jefferson Cade* by BJ James is our MAN OF THE MONTH. In this latest installment of MEN OF BELLE TERRE, the youngest Cade overcomes both external and internal obstacles to regain his lost love. And be sure to read the launch book in Desire's first yearlong continuity series, DYNASTIES: THE CONNELLYS. In *Tall, Dark & Royal*, bestselling author Leanne Banks introduces a prominent Chicago family linked to European royals.

Anne Marie Winston offers another winner with *Billionaire Bachelors: Ryan*, a BABY BANK story featuring twin babies. In *The Tycoon's Temptation* by Katherine Garbera, a jaded billionaire discovers the greater rewards of love, while Kristi Gold's *Dr. Dangerous* discovers he's addicted to a certain physical therapist's personal approach to healing in this launch book of Kristi's MARRYING AN M.D. miniseries. And Metsy Hingle bring us *Navy SEAL Dad*, a BACHELORS & BABIES story.

Start the year off right by savoring all six of these passionate, powerful and provocative romances from Silhouette Desire!

Enjoy!

Joan Marlow Golan

Joan Marlow Golan
Senior Editor, Silhouette Desire

Please address questions and book requests to:
Silhouette Reader Service
U.S.: 3010 Walden Ave., P.O. Box 1325, Buffalo, NY 14269
Canadian: P.O. Box 609, Fort Erie, Ont. L2A 5X3

The Redemption of Jefferson Cade

BJ JAMES

Published by Silhouette Books

America's Publisher of Contemporary Romance

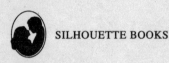 SILHOUETTE BOOKS

ISBN 0-373-76411-1

THE REDEMPTION OF JEFFERSON CADE

Visit Silhouette at www.eHarlequin.com

Printed in U.S.A.

Books by BJ James

Silhouette Desire

The Sound of Goodbye #332
Twice in a Lifetime #396
Shiloh's Promise #529
Winter Morning #595
Slade's Woman #672
A Step Away #692
Tears of the Rose #709
The Man with the
 Midnight Eyes #751
Pride and Promises #789
Another Time, Another Place #823
The Hand of an Angel #844
Heart of the Hunter #945
The Saint of Bourbon Street #951
A Wolf in the Desert #956
†*Whispers in the Dark* #1081
†*Journey's End* #1106
†*Night Music* #1286
‡*The Return of Adams Cade* #1309
‡*A Season for Love* #1335
‡*A Lady for Lincoln Cade* #1369
‡*The Taming of Jackson Cade* #1393
‡*The Redemption of Jefferson Cade* #1411

Silhouette Intimate Moments

Broken Spurs #733

Silhouette Books

World's Most Eligible Bachelors
†*Agent of the Black Watch*

*Men of the Black Watch
†The Black Watch
‡Men of Belle Terre

BJ JAMES'

first book for Silhouette Desire was published in February 1987. Her second Desire novel garnered for BJ a second Maggie, the coveted award of the Georgia Romance Writers. Through the years there have been other awards and nominations for awards, including, from *Romantic Times Magazine,* Reviewer's Choice, Career Achievement, Best Desire and Best Series Romance of the Year. In that time, her books have appeared regularly on a number of bestseller lists, among them Waldenbooks and *USA Today.*

On a personal note, BJ and her physician husband have three sons and two grandsons. While her address reads Mooreboro, this is only the origin of a mail route passing through the countryside. A small village set in the foothills of western North Carolina is her home.

Foreword

In the coastal Lowcountry of South Carolina, where the fresh waters of winding rivers flow into the sea, there is an Eden of unmatched wonders. In this mix of waters and along the shores by which they carve their paths, life is and varied. The land is one of uncommon contrasts, with sandy, sea-swept beaches, mysterious swamps, teeming marshes bounded by ancient maritime forests. And a multitude of creatures abide in each.

In this realm of palms and palmettos, estuaries and rivers, shaded by towering live oaks draped in ghostly Spanish moss, lies Belle Terre. Like an exquisite pearl set among emeralds and sapphires, with its name the small antebellum city describes its province. As it describes itself.

Belle Terre, beautiful land. A beautiful city.

A very proper, very elegant, beautiful city. A gift for the soul. An exquisite mélange for the senses. With ancient and grand structures in varying states of repair and disrepair set along tree-lined, cobbled streets. With narrow, gated gardens lush with such greenery as resurrection and cinnamon ferns. And all of it wrapped in the lingering scent of camellias, azaleas, jessamine and magnolias.

Steeped in an aura of history, its culture and customs influenced by plantations that once abounded in the Lowcountry, as it clings to its past, Belle Terre is a province of contradictions. Within its society one will find arrogance abiding with humility, cruelty with kindness, insolence with gentility, honor with depravity, and hatred with love.

As ever when the senses are whetted and emotions untamed, in Belle Terre there will be passion, romance, and scandal.

Prologue

The wilderness was his sanctuary. As a boy he'd come in search of solace. As a man he came for peace.

From his vantage among the trees, Jefferson Cade looked over a swampy Eden. A land few knew as he knew it. The land of his heart. One of strange, erratic temperament, as now. For even as he waited, its mood altered. Dormant air grew sultry. Moisture permeated each breath and burnished all it touched in a heated mist. The day, and the hideaway tucked among the limbs of the moss strewn tree, were held in the thrall of a lowcountry summer.

Far below the tree house, at the edge of a pond, a fish jumped, startling a fawn just dipping his head to drink. Jefferson smiled as the tiny creature danced away. A smile that vanished as he glimpsed the woman half hidden in the shadow of a palmetto.

Caught by her stillness, he waited. As she watched the fawn, he saw how much she'd changed, yet remained the same. When she'd first come from Argentina to live, to study, and absorb the graces still surviving in the quaint city of Belle Terre, she'd been a girl on the verge of womanhood. Now the tomboy who hunted, fished, and handled horses as well as any man, had indeed become a beautiful woman. And his best friend.

"Marissa." She couldn't have heard, yet her eyes lifted to his. And, as she came to him, he whispered, "Marissa Claire."

A half hour of silence later, Jefferson abandoned his pen and sketch pad. Moving to Marissa's side he sat on the tree house floor, wondering what trouble had drawn her to him.

This meeting had begun strangely. After a subdued greeting and a strained smile, she'd barely spoken. Conversation had never been necessary between them. Yet now her silence was unbearable.

Leaning on an elbow, he stared down at a beguiling woman who lay as if she were sleeping. But he knew her body language too well not to read the wakeful tension. As patience deserted him, he tugged a stray curl. "Hey, lazybones, want to go fishing?"

Reluctantly her dark gaze met his. Knowing the time for pretense was past, but not ready to speak, she looked away.

Jefferson had never seen her so distant. It was rare that she would call him at midday asking that he meet her here. Rare that she barely greeted him then withdrew. Something was wrong. "What is it, Marissa? Why did you ask me to come here?"

When her reply was only a shrug, he lapsed again into silent contemplation. She was Marissa Claire Alexandre. Merrie to all but him, for whom the name hadn't fit. An inexplicable perception he couldn't explain to any but himself.

Four years before, she'd come to Belle Terre. Sent from

the Alexandre *estancia* by a father determined to tame his daredevil daughter. Guided by Eden Cade, Marissa was to learn the ways of Southern ladies. Lessons she'd mastered perfectly, yet never lost her love of country life, or her passion for horses.

In the beginning their friendship was based on mutual admiration of their unique skill with horses. From that beginning came a deepening of common interests. As good friends became confidants, it was to him she turned in happy or troubled times.

But Marissa was only twenty-one, eight years younger than he. A disparity he never forgot, even as the remarkable girl became a remarkable woman—and Jefferson Cade, once forever immune, had fallen deeply in love with her. Deeply but in vain. In denial of all he felt, he survived by reminding himself the woman within the alluring body loved him as a friend.

Too soon even that would be taken from him. From the first, the plan was clear. Marissa would spend five years in her mother's homeland. Then she was to return to Argentina to honor obligations she neither explained nor discussed. Jefferson had learned to live with the inevitable. Time in hand was too precious to waste agonizing over the time to come. And if friendship was all he could have, he would be a friend in every need.

Besieged by desire, but setting the sorrow of it aside, he turned her face to him. "Hey," he questioned as he saw tears in her dark eyes. "What is it, sweetheart? How can I help?"

Marissa stared up at him, memorizing each handsome feature. She knew Jefferson had never understood the charisma of his smile, the power of his kindness. In all their years of friendship, he hadn't known of her dual dilemma. When he'd urged her to spend more time with classmates and teased that she would never find her Prince Charming in the wilds with him, he didn't understand she was promised to a much older man.

A promise she must honor. Though she'd found her prince where Jefferson said she couldn't, she would keep her father's word. And leave her heart in Prince Charming's keeping.

As always in his strong presence, she found her own strength. Catching his wrist, she pressed her cheek in his palm. "There's no help for a day that was preordained. I knew it would come, but not so soon."

Slipping the scarf from her hair, he smoothed dark, silky tresses with his fingers. "What day, Marissa?"

"The day I say goodbye."

He went totally still. "But you have another year."

"That was the agreement. But now it's different." Her voice broke. "I've been called home."

He wondered what agreement, but only asked, "When?"

Tears she'd denied flooded her eyes. "I leave tomorrow."

Jefferson tensed. Then he drew her to him, embracing her in futile denial. "Not yet. Not so soon."

Her arms crept around him, her head rested over his heart. She would remember this moment and treasure it. Someday she would tell the children she might have about this enchanting place, and of the man whose creation the tree house had been.

If she had sons, she would speak of his ruggedness, his adventures, and his communion with the wilderness. If she had daughters, she would tell them of the tenderness of a beautiful man, and would wonder if they looked into her heart and saw the truth.

But that lay in the future, that didn't begin until tomorrow. Until then, she had this one, last day with Jefferson.

His chest rose and fell beneath her cheek as it nestled

against the hard muscles. His hands at her shoulders moved her from his embrace. His shadowed stare moved over her face, lingering at her mouth, her eyes. Seeing what he hadn't let himself see before. Believing what he hadn't dared believe.

"Dear God," he whispered, with regret for lost time, lost love.

Marissa didn't flinch or turn away. For once, she wouldn't hide what she felt for him.

Jefferson's heart filled with hope. "Don't go, Marissa." Softly he spoke words he never expected to say. "Stay with me."

In his face she saw despair, honor, a friend's love. With a sigh she spoke the truth. "I can't. There is a man, my father owes him a great deal. In return, I was promised to him long ago."

"Promised to him?" Whatever he expected, it was never this. "Do you love him? Have I misread what I see in your eyes?"

Marissa felt the lash of his anger and forgave it. "I hardly know him. The betrothal was a business arrangement. He wanted a wife one day. It was decided I would be that wife."

"In return for what?" Jefferson's clasp on her shoulders seared into her flesh. "What do you get out of this arrangement?"

"I get nothing, Jefferson. But because of me, my father and mother can keep their life as it is."

"Your life and you were traded for wealth, to insure a lifestyle?" He spat the words. "Your father would do that?"

"For money, power, the lifestyle? Yes." Marissa was calm beneath his angry glare. "It's the way of the wealthy, bartering lives, love, even children. My father was desperate. My mother's health was failing. It was for her sake he negotiated this time in Belle Terre. In the bargain, I was to bring the expected graces to the marriage. And who better than Eden to teach me? Now, as a point of honor, my father is impatient to resolve the debt.''

''Honor?'' Disgust seethed in Jefferson. Disgust she didn't deserve. She loved her mother and her father. She was so young at the time, what choice was there for her? Deep in his soul, he understood. But understanding couldn't ease the anguish.

''Arranged marriages aren't uncommon in my land and families like mine. All my father has ever known is abundant wealth. As young as I was, even I could see the more extravagant the lifestyle, the less one can fathom living a lesser existence. In your world, the arrangement is despicable. In my father's, he has done his best for his family. I could defy him and refuse to honor his word. But, because my mother's illness is slowly debilitating and will likely continue for years, I won't try.''

Jefferson drew a breath. An unsteady hand caressed her face. Softly, he said, ''Then tell me how I can help you now.''

Marissa's lips brushed the heel of his hand. Her steady gaze held his. ''You could make love to me.''

His chest felt like a vise. If his mind reeled, now it spun into dementia. ''No,'' he heard himself say, though there was nothing he wanted more than to make love to her. ''You don't know what you're asking. You haven't considered the repercussions.''

''You're wrong, my dearest friend. I know exactly what I'm asking. I've considered every repercussion. What I'm expected to do, what I will do, is for my family.'' Touching his face, she let her drifting fingertips linger at his mouth. ''This, I ask for me.''

Curling her fingers into a fist, she stared at her hand, and thought of his. Strong, hard, roughened by calluses, yet beautiful. And even in passion his touch would be gentle.

"What crime is it to learn of love from a man who cares? What sin to want you, Jefferson? I do, you know," she whispered.

Jefferson clung to one last shred of sanity. "You…"

"Don't!" A fingertip stopped his words. "Don't tell me I don't know what I want, what I need. You haven't misread anything and I'm not asking for forever. But for my first time, I need to feel your hands on my body. Only yours.

"I can't change the path of my life. But I can survive it if you give me this to remember. If you pretend for a little while that you love me as more than a friend."

"No." Though he drew away from her and rose to stand at his full height, he meant only that he wouldn't be pretending. Marissa didn't understand. As hurt gathered the eyes, right or wrong, he knew he couldn't deny her. Or himself.

There was so much more he wanted to say, but he couldn't think. He couldn't be wise or pragmatic. He could only love her.

"Marissa." He called her name, only her name. Yet beneath the storm of emotions lay an unspoken question as his slowly extended hand offered her a chance to back away. His riveted look moved from his own roughened fingers to her face. As a bewildered frown marred her brow, he spoke again. "Take my hand, sweetheart. But only if you truly want me. Only if you're sure."

In a subtle change, hope shone in her eyes. "I'm sure, Jefferson." As she took his hand, her resolve was strong. "I've never been more sure in my life."

As clasped hands held fast, drawing her up to his embrace, he knew there were questions to ask. Warnings to give. But common sense was lost as he reveled in holding her. Then into his own silence, he breathed a surrendering word. A curse? A prayer? Not even Jefferson knew. The battle was done. There was no going back.

In the stillness he undressed her, and the discarding of each garment became an exquisite seduction. Each button slipped free, unveiling her body inch by inch, inviting a touch, a kiss.

When she was cloaked only in sun-spangled shadows and the dark cascade of her hair, he discovered she was more beautiful than he'd dreamed. More desirable. With a final caress, his hands fell away to attend the task of undressing himself.

When the last of his own clothing was cast away, seeing the apprehension of innocence, taking her hands in his, he brought them to his mouth. Lips and breath warming her cold fingers, he murmured, "Don't be afraid, Marissa."

Bringing her nearer, he bent to kiss the tender flesh beneath her ear. As she murmured an indistinct sound of pleasure, he let his fingertips stray over her throat and down. When his hands closed over her breasts, his palms teasing their tips, the nipples hardened, as his own body had, with desire.

"Don't be afraid," he said one last time.

Marissa's answer was a whisper as he drew her down to the floor. "Never with you, Jefferson." When his lips followed the path of his touch she cried again, "Never with you."

A virile man, Jefferson was far from innocent. He knew how to tantalize, how to excite, as he took Marissa with him from one degree of longing to another. Erotic forays discovered where to stroke, when to kiss, when to suckle, leaving her desperate for more, yet wondering how there could ever be. Then he tapped a secret well of unthinking hunger that spiraled into impassioned madness, intensifying every need.

Always before, he was the sole maker of madness. Once passion had sufficed. But with the coherent thought he could manage beneath her touch, he knew passion for passion's sake would never be enough again. And, as he found himself falling deeper beneath her spell, nor would anyone but Marissa.

He'd never wanted forever. He wanted it now. But in its stead, he would make for her a beautiful memory to take to a new life. And for himself, a dream. The only forever he could have.

Swept into the madness, a gentle man became more gentle. When she called his name in a voice husky with desire, there was no past, no future. They were only a man and a woman trembling on the edge of a world where neither had gone, and would never go again.

Drawing away, he looked down at her. "Even the making of a beautiful memory can be painful. But only once." Sealing his promise with a kiss, he came down to her, whispering, "Only once."

In a day bright and hot, a cry sounded as moisture laden air painted joining bodies in a sheen of gossamer. Then there was only a sigh of welcome as Jefferson went with Marissa into the last of rapture...while the world waited.

The splash wasn't enough to wake him, but it did. As naturally as breathing, he reached for Marissa. He was alone. In her place lay the scarf he'd taken from her hair. Sliding on his jeans, he moved to the ladder that led to the ground.

"No," Marissa called from the water's edge. "Don't come down, Jefferson. I don't think I could bear to leave if you do."

"Don't go," he pleaded, though he knew it was futile.

Marissa didn't answer. As he stopped short of the first rung, she turned to toss a stone into the pond. The water's surface was calm before she spoke again. "This day and this place have been magic. So I thought the pond could be a wishing well. It was greedy of me, but I've made two wishes."

"What did you wish, Marissa?"

When she looked up at him, her smile was bittersweet. "First I wished you wouldn't forget me."

Jefferson said nothing. It was a wish already granted. How could a man forget a woman like Marissa? "And the second?"

"The impossible."

"Maybe it doesn't have to be, sweetheart."

Her smile faltered. "You're wrong, my beloved friend. Though I've wished with all my heart, how could we meet again?"

A knife in his heart couldn't hurt as much. "Wishing wells grant three wishes. Will you wish again?"

"Yes." The stone was already in her hand.

"Will you tell me the last?"

"Not this time. Not this wish."

Jefferson didn't pry. And though he knew what would follow the splash of the last stone, he wasn't ready for it.

"Goodbye, Jefferson Cade." Her voice was soft, her words halting. "I won't forget you. I won't forget this day."

"Marissa." He waited until she turned back, until their eyes met. "If ever you need me…I'll come for you."

"I know," she acknowledged and turned away again.

He wanted to call out to her, to ask her again to stay. Instead, as silent as the wilderness, he watched her go.

At the far shore, she stopped and raised a hand. It was then the storm for which the land waited lashed out in a blinding bolt of lightning and a rumble of thunder. When the world was quiet again, the path was empty. Marissa had gone from his life.

* * *

Heavy rain was falling when Jefferson paused at the edge of the clearing. Through the downpour, his gaze sought the half-hidden bower where he'd made love to Marissa Claire Alexandre.

His sketch pad shielded by his body, a keepsake folded against his heart, he committed to memory this place. He would paint it, melding sketches and memories. Someday.

Rain fell harder, spattering over the pond like stones in a wishing well. "One wish is true, Marissa."

Lightning flickered, thunder growled. As quickly as it came, the rain stopped. As a mist shrouded the land, Jefferson waited for one more glimpse that never came. It didn't matter.

"I won't forget."

When he turned away, though the wilderness had been an abiding part of his life, he knew it could never be the same.

He wouldn't come again.

One

―――

"**W**ell, hello, handsome." The greeting, addressing the lone patron at the bar, was lilting and feminine. Teasing a favorite customer.

Setting his glass aside, a hand automatically going to his Stetson, Jefferson Cade smiled. A brush of his fingers tilting the tan brim accompanied a pleasant greeting as teasing. "Afternoon, Miss Cristal."

As she laughed in pleasure at the Western gallantry spoken in a Southern drawl, Cristal Lane slipped her arm through his. "What brings a Southern gentleman like you into town today?"

In this land of old ranches and older family names, with time measured in half centuries, if not centuries, Cristal was counted as new to Arizona. But Jefferson considered the remark conversation, not a question, for she'd owned the most popular saloon in Silverton years enough to know the spring stock show held annually in the town attracted ranchers from miles around. As it had drawn him from the Broken Spur of Sunrise Canyon.

But Cristal was also familiar enough with his reclusive lifestyle to believe the show, itself, would not merit one of his rare visits. As she silently signaled for the bartender to refresh the drink he'd hardly touched, Jefferson wasn't surprised when she suggested, quietly, "Someone must be offering a spectacular horse to tempt you from your hideout."

"Think so?" Shifting his gaze from her, he nodded his thanks to the bartender, then folded his hands around the glass.

Her shrewd study drifted away to assess the needs of customers. Satisfied everyone was content, she looked again at the handsome Southerner, and inevitably at his hands.

As with everything about Jefferson Cade, his hands were intriguing. Weathered, callused, the hands of a working man, an artist. A mix of rugged elegance and gentle strength. One of the times he'd been in town and stayed late to walk her home after closing, she'd teased him about his hands. He'd only laughed when she'd called them fascinating, saying it was natural that any living, breathing female would wonder about his touch.

He'd asked what female? For in the four years since he'd returned to Arizona to work for Jake Benedict at the Rafter B, then Steve Cody at the Broken Spur, he'd done no more than speak a few pleasantries to any woman. Beyond the routine associations of ranching, he was happiest living his reclusive life.

"Do I think so? Yes," she murmured to his reflection in the mirror behind the bar. "It must be one helluva horse."

Her use of the rare profanity recalled a late-night talk when she'd ventured another startling opinion.

It must've been one helluva woman who spoiled all the rest of womankind for you, Jefferson Cade. She'd made the statement, then never mentioned it again. But he knew she was remembering the night and her words as her eyes probed his.

Jefferson held her gaze for a long moment, then turned his face away. A virile face maturity had made more attractive, and the new touch of silver in his dark blond hair only complemented. His mouth was solemn now. Beneath the brim of the Stetson, his downswept lashes shielded his eyes. But if his head had lifted and if his lips tilted in a smile that touched his eyes, it would still make an attractive man startlingly handsome.

He was immune, not a fool. He knew he'd caught the attention of a number of the female population of Silverton in the early days of his return. But he never acknowledged the most blatant flirtation with more than a courtly smile and a pleasant greeting. He became a master at making the most brazen feel he was flattered and perplexed by the advances, a gallantry that, at first, had an opposite effect than the one he wanted. But through the years, as even the most determined found him ever elusive, his would-be lovers became friendly acquaintances, if not friends.

Though she teased about his charm, Cristal's interest was platonic. As he recognized her honesty and wisdom, she became a close friend. A rare and trusted confidante.

"If not for a particular horse, you wouldn't be here, would you, Jefferson? There's nothing else in your life. You won't let there be, because of a woman." Cristal voiced a long-standing concern, exercising the privilege of friendship.

Only the narrowing of his eyes signaled this subject was off-limits. For once, Cristal wasn't to be deterred. "Do you ever get her out of your mind or your heart? This woman you loved and lost…do you ever stop thinking about her? Can you stop? Or do you spend each waking moment remembering how she looked, how she smiled, the way she walked? The fragrance of her hair?''

Jefferson didn't respond. Then, pushing away from the bar, his expression unreadable, he looked down at her. ''What I'm thinking and remembering,'' he said as courteously as if she weren't prying, ''is that it's time to see a man about a horse.''

Fingers at his hat brim, a charming smile, a low, ''Miss Cristal,'' and she was left to watch him walk away. Long after he stepped through the door and disappeared into the crowd, no less concerned she stared at the space where he'd been.

''Cristal,'' a raucous voice called. ''How about a song?''

''Sure, Hal.'' She didn't need to look around to recognize a regular customer. ''What would you like to hear?''

''No preference, honey,'' he answered. ''Just sing.''

With a last glance at the empty doorway, Cristal crossed the room. Despite the tightening in her throat, leaning over the piano player, aptly named Sam, she whispered in his ear. When he nodded, she looked over the room, her smile touched with sadness for a lonely man. ''How about this one? An oldie for a friend.''

As the melancholy chords of the introduction ended, wondering what intuition dictated the old tune, she sang of a lady's choice to leave the man who loved her.

''Easy girl. Nobody's going to hurt you. Not anymore.'' In a soothing singsong, Jefferson coaxed the nervous mare from the trailer. As she stepped down the ramp, ears flicking in suspicion, he didn't blame her. Even for a high-strung filly who hadn't been mishandled, the unfamiliar surroundings and the noise of the stock show would've been excuse enough for being skittish.

When she'd come on the market as a difficult horse offered at a nominal fee, the most uninformed judge of horses could see promise. Which, given the bargain price, sent up a red flag that warned labeling her difficult was an understatement. Jefferson had driven to her home stable for a preliminary look, taking Sandy Gannon, foreman of the Rafter B and an expert judge of horses, with him for a second opinion. Both agreed the filly was of a bloodline and a quality Steve Cody would approve.

When the seller questioned who could tame the filly, Sandy replied that if Jeff Cade couldn't, then it couldn't be done.

"Let's hope Sandy knows what he's talking about," Jefferson crooned to the filly when she finally stood on the ground. The truth was, Sandy knew exactly what he was saying when he praised the Southerner. Before assuming duties at the Broken Spur, Jefferson had spent the last two of three years at the Rafter B as second in command. Though he'd made a show of grumbling over losing a good horseman, Sandy had backed Steve and his wife Savannah's choice.

Now, Jefferson had lived and worked in Sunrise Canyon for more than a year, loving each solitary day. "So will you, girl," he promised as he led the filly to a stall. "Some folks think it's lonely in the canyon, but it isn't. You'll see."

Realizing he was talking to a horse that would run with Steve's small herd, he laughed. A sound too rare in his life. "A stranger would think the loneliness has driven me bonkers. When it's driven me a little saner, instead."

His string of chatter elicited a low whinny and a nudge, and he knew his faith in the filly hadn't been misplaced. Stroking her, he murmured, "You'll be happy here, girl. One day soon, when we know what fits, we'll choose a name for you."

Slipping a bar over the stall door, he made a quick check of the other horses and stepped outside. After a long day and a four-hour drive across the surrounding Benedict land, it was good to steal a minute to watch the moon rise.

In daylight or darkness, the canyon was beautiful. When he'd come to Arizona as a teenage runaway he'd been too young and his life too chaotic to appreciate the stark magnificence of the land. Ten years later, when he'd left the lowcountry again—running away as an adult—he hadn't expected to find anything to equal the lovely land he left behind.

He was wrong. As an adult with an artist's eye, he recognized the different degrees of beauty, the different kinds.

The desert was his home now. Though he knew he could never go back, the lowcountry had been in his mind recently. Perhaps because, after years of neglect, he'd taken out his sketches and in the long winter darkness, he'd begun to paint again.

A painting waited now on the easel. The light wasn't so good in the renovated cabin, but it didn't matter. Painting was something he did for himself. A final healing, an exorcism.

Abandoning the soothing sight of the canyon in moonlight, he returned to the truck to retrieve his mail. No one wrote to him but family. Though he treasured the snapshots and letters, days could pass before he made a mail run. Given the size of the packet the postmaster'd had waiting for him, the time had been even longer.

Jefferson cared deeply for his brothers, and he was never truly out of touch. The family knew to contact the Rafter B in emergencies. Sandy would relay any messages by telephone or rider. No phone calls, no rider meant everyone was well and safe.

Tucking the packet under his arm, as the door of the truck closed, he whistled. Two clear notes sounded in the failing light, answered by a bark and the pad of racing feet.

As he braced himself, a dark shape launched itself like a bullet at his chest.

Letters scattered in the dust as Jefferson went down. A massive creature blacker than the night stood over him. Gleaming teeth bared in a grin, a long, pink tongue lapped at his face.

Laughing, pushing the great dog aside, Jefferson muttered, "If that means you're glad to see me, Satan, I hope you won't be quite so glad next time."

Satan barked and danced away. Normally with his sentry duty done, he was ready to play. This night, as if he would hurry his master to abandon the game by helping him to stand, the dog grabbed his hand between his teeth. The slightest pressure could have caused injury but, as with all creatures trained by Jefferson, despite his fierce look Satan was as gentle as his master.

The mock attack was a game, begun when Jefferson was new to the canyon and Satan a puppy with too much energy. Soon the dog should be taught the game was too dangerous. "Someone could misunderstand and put a bullet in your head." Jefferson cuffed him gently in a signal to let go. "Might bend the bullet."

Satan trotted away again in the prance common to Doberman pinschers everywhere. Stopping short, his dark eyes on his master's face, he made a sound Jefferson interpreted as canine impatience.

"Not funny?" Rising, the human side of the conversation dusted off his clothes. Gathering the mail, he declared in an understatement, "Considering that I would miss you, tonight's a good time to stop the game. As you obviously have."

In the gloom settling over the canyon, he almost missed one piece of mail. Satan's pawing interest, combined with the dull glint of its metal clasp caught his attention. Without both, the brown envelope would have blended with the shadowed Arizona dust. Perhaps to be discovered in morning light. Perhaps not.

Hefting it, he judged its weight. More than a letter, with only a blurred postmark. No return address. "What could this be?"

Satan barked and paced toward the cabin. "You're right," Jefferson agreed. "I should go inside and have a look."

Normally the Doberman refused to come inside. Tonight, he slipped past Jefferson when the door opened. Rather than stretching out on the hearth as usual in his rare sorties in the cabin, he streaked through the main room to the bedroom.

"Come away, Satan," Jefferson scolded as the dog scratched at the bedside table. "There's nothing here."

Nothing but a keepsake from his past, Jefferson amended as he herded the dog from the room. "Lie by the hearth," he directed. "After I check the mail, we'll have supper."

Satan obeyed, instantly. Containing his agitation, he tucked his nose beneath his paws. His dark eyes were white-rimmed beneath the pupils as he tracked each move his master made.

Jefferson sat at the table. Spreading mail over it, he plucked the brown envelope from the jumble. Satan whimpered. "Hey." Jefferson moved it left, then right. Only Satan's eyes turned, never leaving the letter. "What about this worries you?"

Jefferson believed animals possessed unique senses, perceiving more than the human mind could begin to conceive. Some would laugh, others would scoff at the idea, but he'd seen this anticipation too often in the wilderness to not believe it.

He'd seen it before in Satan when a rattler had crawled into a stall, striking a colt. Though little more than a pup, the dog had clawed at the cabin door, waking Jefferson, demanding his attention. Then he'd torn a pair of jeans as he'd dragged his master to the barn. Because of Satan, the colt was alive. Because of Satan, Jefferson opened the envelope with trepidation.

"What the devil?" he tore open another envelope.

When he moved past the surprise of discovering one unmarked envelope inside another, he almost pitched the whole package in the trash as a joke. Recalling Satan's reaction, he continued.

The next envelope, the last, bore a name. His name, written in a hand he knew. For one stunned moment he thought it was a cruel hoax. Next he questioned how it could be. When he drew out two sheets of paper, he knew it wasn't. The first was newspaper. The second a plain, white sheet torn raggedly from a tablet. One line was written across the sheet in the same familiar hand.

His own hand shaking, for longer than he knew, Jefferson stared down at it, tracing each letter, each word, with his startled gaze. Catching an unsteady breath, an unforgettable fragrance filling his lungs, touching his heart, he read the written words out loud. His own words, spoken just once, long ago.

If ever you need me…

A promise made. A promise to keep. But how?

The answer lay in the second sheet. A month-old newspaper article. "'The search for the plane of Paulo Rei has been terminated,'" he read, then read again. "'On board were Señor Rei, his wife, the former Marissa Claire Alexandre, and her parents.'"

There was more, a detailed description of the Reis and their lives. But Jefferson's voice stumbled to a halt. Papers fluttered to the floor. As his gaze lifted to the portrait over the mantel, he recited the only line that mattered in a lifeless voice, "'It has been determined there could be no survivors.'"

No survivors. The words were a cry in his mind. Words that made no sense. Trying to find sanity in it, he read his own words again. A promise only Marissa would know.

But a part of him couldn't comprehend or separate truth from fiction. Was it a charade? A ghoulish trick? Or was it real?

If it was real, why was it assumed Marissa had been on the plane? If it wasn't she who had sent the letter, then who?

His thoughts were a whirligig, going 'round and 'round, always ending in the same place, the same thought, the same denial. No one but Marissa could have sent the letter. It had to be. It must be. For, if she hadn't, it would mean she was dead.

"No!" Jefferson refused to believe. "I would know. The world wouldn't feel right without Marissa."

But how could he be sure? How could he know he wasn't persuading himself to believe what he needed to believe?

"Satan!" The name was spoken without thought or conscious volition. But as he heard it, Jefferson knew it was the way. Rigid as stone, the dog had watched. Now he came to attention, awaiting the command that always followed his name spoken in that tone. Jefferson smiled, a humorless tilt of his lips. Recognizing the stance, he gave the expected command. "Stay."

Certain Satan would obey, he returned to his bedroom. Opening the drawer by the bedside table, he drew out a scarf. A square of silk filled with memories.

Marissa's scarf. A memento of a day never forgotten.

How many times had he seen her wear it? How often had he thought how pretty the bright color was lying against her nape, holding back her dark hair? Why, when he wanted to so badly, had he never dared fling it away to wrap himself in the spill of silken locks?

How could her perfume linger so long, a reminder of the day he'd lived the dream he hadn't dared?

"The day I made love to Marissa."

As the floodgates opened, memories he'd never allowed himself to dwell on came rushing in wistful vignettes....

Marissa riding as only Marissa could, her body moving in perfect harmony with the horse.

Marissa with a rifle in her hand, the dedicated hunter who could track anything, but could never pull the trigger.

Marissa picking an orchid to celebrate sighting an eagle.

Marissa that last day. Sad, solemn, walking through sunlight and shadow to come to him. The wistful woman he'd loved for longer than he would admit, wanting him, as he'd wanted her.

Marissa, the innocent, teaching him what love should be. Wishing he couldn't forget her, and that they would meet again. Leaving with a wish unspoken, a secret he would never know.

Marissa, her hand raised in farewell, disappearing in the blinding furor of a storm.

"Dear God." Jefferson clutched the scarf. Every moment he'd locked away in the back of his mind was as fresh, as real as the day it happened. Though he truly couldn't forget on a subconscious level, he'd thought time had eased the bittersweet ache of mingled pain and joy. Proof in point, the portrait of Marissa hanging over the cabin's single fireplace.

The painting had been a satisfying exercise, one he believed had leeched away regrets, pain, longing.

"Fool." It would never end. Cristal's shot in the dark was more intuitive than he'd let himself admit. No matter the games he played, no matter how deeply he hid his head in the sand, what he felt for Marissa was too vibrant to tame into memory.

As the guilt that plagued him for his part in sending his

brother Adams to prison, never truly eased. Guilt that ruled and changed his life. Because of his teenage folly and what it had taken from Adams, he was never quite at home with his own family. His peace and refuge was the swamp. Then came the hurt of losing Marissa, and even the swamp was no longer a place of peace.

"Losing her made it all too..." Jefferson didn't have the right word. Nothing was quite enough. Lashes drifting briefly to his cheeks, he stood remembering regret, help-lessness. Pain.

"Too much," he whispered, understanding at last. He'd never analyzed the truth of why he'd fled the lowcountry the second time. He knew now it had been because of a morass of unresolved guilt and loss and grief. Arizona offered solitude, a different sort of peace. Here there was no one to hurt. No one to lose. No one he might fail. "Until now," he said softly. "If this is Marissa."

It was. He knew it in his very soul. But an expert second opinion wouldn't hurt. "Come, Satan."

With a surge of impatience, he barely waited for the dog to stand obediently by his side. Bending down, he held the scarf before the sensitive black nose. "Fetch."

The Doberman bounded away. Jefferson had barely moved to the doorway, when Satan returned. The page from a tablet was clasped in his mouth. Taking it from the sharp teeth, praising the dog with a stroking touch, Jefferson knew Satan's instincts, and his, had been vindicated. The scent that lingered on the scarf and the message was the same.

Marissa was alive.

Stunned, his mind a morass of grief and relief—relief that she was alive, grief for all she'd been through, all she'd lost—he couldn't think. Like a sleepwalker, he returned to the table and sat down. How long he sat there, staring up at Marissa's portrait, he would never know. Time had no meaning. Nothing mattered but that Marissa was alive.

"Why contact me, sweetheart? Why in such troubled times?" The sound of his own voice was a wake-up call. Suddenly, as with a man who lived by his wits, his mind was keen, perceptive, and considering each point and question. The most important was answered by his own promise. This was more than the call of grief.

If ever you need me... "I'll come for you," he finished. A promise recalled, but deliberately left unsaid.

Marissa was alive. Given the subterfuge of the message, she was in danger. She needed help. She needed Jefferson Cade. "But where are you, sweetheart? What clue did you..." His voice stumbled as he remembered the scrap of newspaper falling to the floor. Instinct told him he would find the answers there.

Minutes later, Jefferson was on the telephone that had gathered dust during his tenure at the Broken Spur. In rare impatience, he paced back and forth as far as the cord would allow while he waited for his call to be put through.

When Jericho Rivers, sheriff of Belle Terre, responded, Jefferson spoke tersely. "I'm coming to the lowcountry, to Belle Terre. I need to meet with you and Yancey Hamilton."

Jericho was known for his instincts and Jefferson was grateful for them now. Perhaps it was his tone, that he had called the sheriff rather than his own brothers, or simply that he was returning to Belle Terre, but for whatever reason, the sheriff only asked the particulars—when, where, how soon—and no more.

One step had been taken, leaving two more in the form of local calls. One to Sandy Gannon that would elicit no more questions than the call to Jericho. Jefferson trusted both men to do what was needed, when, and for however long.

The final call was to the airlines. The first stage of his arrangements was complete when he sat before a fireplace without fire. A letter had changed his brother Lincoln's life. Now a letter had done the same for his. Laying a hand on the Doberman's dark head, he muttered, "Sandy's sending someone to look after the ranch and you. But I'll be back, Satan. I don't know when, or what will have changed, but I'll be back."

On a windswept plain, a solitary woman walked through a waking world. Wind tore at her clothes and tangled in her hair, but she didn't notice. Had she noticed, she wouldn't care.

Once she'd been at home and happy in this sparsely populated land. A place of towering mountains and endless deserts, of sprawling plains and rocky coastlines. Once she'd loved the still beauty of wild places sheltered from the wind. Once she'd waited in wonder for that moment when birdsong heralded the incipient day, then fell silent in the breathless trembling time when the sun lifted above distant, wind-scoured hills and bathed the world in a shower of light.

Once she'd loved so many things about this land. Now as she walked, cloaked in a mantle of solitude, waiting for another day that would be no more to her than simply another day, her sense of aloneness intensified. There was no beauty for her grief-stricken eyes. No serenity in a serene world. Not for her.

Never again for Marissa Claire Alexandre Rei in this land called Silver by the first conquistadores.

"Argentina," she whispered as she paused in this sleepless hour, to stare at an untamed plain that in the half light had no beginning, no end. "A land of grief and loss."

A hand closed over her shoulder, its warmth driving away the chill of the wind. "Are you all right, little Rissa?"

His voice was deep and quiet, his English excellent and only a little accented by the speech patterns of Spanish, his first language. His touch hadn't startled her. Before he'd spoken, she'd known he had come to join her. "I'm fine, Juan." Her brown eyes, turned black in the paling of dawn, met eyes as black. "Fine."

"Who do you convince, *querida?*" he asked gently as his hand moved from her shoulder. "Yourself, or me?"

She laughed, a bleak sound. "Obviously no one."

"You walk now because you don't sleep," Juan suggested, moving with her as she began to walk again. "Not because you love the land at dawn as you once did."

Marissa didn't speak. She didn't look at this man she'd known all her life. The first to take her up on a horse, when he was in his teens and she was five. He was the first to instill in her a love of horses and riding. Juan Elia was a modern-day gaucho. A true descendant of Argentina's famed, wandering horsemen. With the coming of the *estancias,* the ranches, the wandering had ceased. Gauchos had settled down to work for the families of the *estancias,* as the Elia family had worked for countless years for her father's family. The life of the gaucho had changed, but the indomitable spirit hadn't been lost, nor the horsemanship.

Nor the loyalty that kept him here in a secret camp on the plain, rather than at home with his wife and three-year-old son.

"It isn't the same," she answered at last. "Nothing is as it was in the days when you brought me here as a young girl. When we rode like Cossacks over the plain."

"In the days when you wanted to be a real gaucho and wander the land?" Juan chuckled. "Before your mother and father sent you to the United States to become a Southern lady."

"Does growing up tarnish everything, Juan?"

He stopped her then. A touch at her cheek turned her to him. The sun was just lifting over the crest of a hill, in the sudden sliver of light his Native American heritage was visible in a face that had gown more handsome with time. "Death and guilt have tarnished this land for you. Deaths you couldn't prevent. Guilt you shouldn't bear."

"I was supposed to be on that plane."

"But, because of a sick child, *my* child, you weren't. You didn't send your mother and your father and your husband to their deaths, *querida*. Whoever planted the bomb did that."

"Because the plane disappeared off radar so abruptly doesn't mean it was a bomb." Marissa didn't want to believe explosives had blasted her husband's plane from the sky. Believing would lay the blame even more irrevocably at her door.

"*I* know," Juan said adamantly. "Just as I know who." Softly, he added, "As I know why."

"No." Marissa tried to turn away. Juan wouldn't let her.

"This is no more your fault than any of the rest. You were married to a man more than twice your age. If love was lacking, loyalty was not. You have no reason to accuse yourself.

"If a man of power covets all your husband has, his business, his land, his wife, the sin isn't yours. If he tries to coerce your husband to become a part of something evil, it isn't your fault. If this man decrees all you love and you must be punished for being honorable and loyal to the principles of a lifetime, it isn't your dishonor. If he carries out his threat in a way most horrible, the crime is his, not yours.

"My child lives because of your goodness. Your family died at the hand of an evil man. There is no connection."

"That a bomb caused the crash was a passing speculation, dismissed as quickly," Marissa reminded him.

"Yes," Juan admitted. "But there was the threat. And all who knew have been silenced. Or so he believes."

"Then, if Menendez should discover I'm alive, that would mean he would also have discovered you've hidden me and given me shelter. What more proof would he need to suspect you know everything? Then, my dear friend, your life would be at risk, as well." Fear trembled in her voice for this trusted man who was more like a cherished brother than a friend.

"No, *querida*," Juan soothed. "To the world, I am merely a gaucho who lived and worked on your father's *estancia*. Who would suspect an enduring friendship begun between a girl of five and a boy of sixteen? Who would believe such a grand lady as Señora Rei helped to bring my long-awaited first child into the world. Or that the name he bears is in her honor?"

"But if they should..."

"You will be gone from here long before that could happen. And when you're gone, we'll be as we were. My Marta, Alejandro, and I," he promised. "And you, Rissa? You will be safe."

Marissa brushed a forearm across her brow as if she would shield eyes that had known too many tears. "Will Jefferson come? After so long will he remember a promise? Will he care?"

"If he is even half the man you spoke of, he will remember, he will care, and he will come."

"We can't be sure he got a message passed through so many hands. If he did, was it too cryptic? The article on the back of the newspaper may mean nothing to him. He might not read it."

"He will read it, *querida*. He will read each word over and over again. Because he knows he must understand, he won't stop until he does. He will see the marks and make

words of them. Then, he will come to the *estancia,* and
Marta will do the rest.''

"After that can you be safe, Juan? You or your family?''

"Yes,'' he assured her as he smiled at a secret thought.

*We will be safe and you, Marissa, will be in the arms of
the man you love, at last.*

Two

"**W**hat the hell is this about?"

If Jefferson expected an answer, the buffeting thunder of the helicopter would have made it incomprehensible. With it, the pilot who had introduced himself as Rick Cahill and a friend of Jericho Rivers's, though courteous and efficient, was closemouthed. His eyes, cold steel, never wavered from the sky.

As he'd watched the helicopter fly fast and low through the canyon at dawn, Jefferson had known it was in the hands of an expert. When the monstrous machine touched down as gently as a dragonfly, he suspected the pilot could fly anything, anywhere.

"With his eyes closed." The growled assessment drew the pilot's attention. A riveting gaze turned. A lifted brow as black as shorn, curling hair, was the only variant in a calm expression.

Leaving his silence unbroken, Jefferson answered the

question in those keen eyes with a shrug and looked away. But not before he wondered again at the strange turn of events.

Within hours of opening Marissa's cryptic message, his ordered life had spiraled into quiet chaos. Plans made, airline reservations secured, the ranch bedded down for the night, he'd been packing a duffel when the telephone rang. Alarmed, he'd answered abruptly. The caller's voice was familiar, stunned recognition came with Billy Blackhawk's official preamble and statement of the purpose of his call. Though the sheriff of Silverton was far from a stranger, Jefferson would have questioned the message he'd relayed, were it not for his mention of Jericho.

Even then, he'd found it difficult to forego questions. But on the strength of Jericho's name and Billy Blackhawk's reputation, he had. Billy's promise that everything would be explained when he arrived at an undisclosed destination didn't ease his wariness. An astute judgment warned that questioning Rick Cahill would be useless. Preserving the silence between them, Jefferson stared out the window. That the helicopter was capable of astonishing speeds was evident. As they flew toward the sun and deeper into the day, one color of the earth segued into another in the blink of an eye.

When the chopper landed on an isolated airfield, Jefferson assumed it was to refuel. Instead, Cahill tossed the duffel to the tarmac, signaled his passenger should follow, and climbed from the cockpit.

In a ground-eating jog, Cahill approached the hangar. With a scarred hand, he signaled Jefferson to wait while he entered a small door and disappeared inside. Sooner than anticipated, the hangar doors rumbled open, and Cahill stepped out, a grin turning the steel of his eyes to smoke. "We made it."

"Made what?" Jefferson asked as he joined Cahill.

"This destination, undisturbed. Which we hope means no one traced the letter to you or the Broken Spur."

"Undisturbed." Blue eyes narrowed. "By whom? Why?"

Cahill's grin faded. "The same people who shot Paulo Rei's plane out of the sky. *Why* can be better answered when we reach our final destination."

Shuddering in renewed horror, Jefferson kept silent.

"The crew will be back shortly. To return the chopper to its owner, now that its maintenance is finished." Another grin ghosted over the pilot's lips. "We should be gone before then."

"In that." Jefferson spoke of a small jet. "Which, I suppose, has been sent for maintenance that will never take place."

"Actually, the jet is for sale. The prospective buyer has taken it for a test flight and evaluation."

Jefferson nodded. "Too bad he isn't going to buy."

"Yeah." Respect gleamed in Cahill's eyes.

In the air, Rick Cahill was less guarded, but just as intent. While the jet streaked toward the east and a clandestine meeting, Jefferson thought of a plane the world assumed Marissa was aboard. And that Rick claimed had been blasted from the sky.

Questions teemed in Jefferson's mind. They went unvoiced. When the jet was traded for another helicopter, time zones had been crossed and daylight had burned away like a candle. But the terrain was green and mountainous now. He needed no answers to know this was the last of a convoluted journey.

Rick flew with the same skill and concentration, skimming through mountain passes as he followed the snaking path of a river. At a waterfall he banked and climbed, then dropped into a valley crisscrossed by creeks and a river filled by another waterfall. The tin roofs of two buildings gleamed in the sun. The helicopter hovered, then set down with an ease that recalled the canyon landing.

Jericho was there, flanked by Simon McKinzie whom Jefferson had met only once. Tall and massive, a lean Goliath whose mix of French and Native American heritage was evident in his chiseled features and gleaming black hair, the sheriff should have dwarfed the older man. But on the strength of that single meeting at Jericho's wedding, Jefferson had discovered no one could overshadow the silver-haired, bull-shouldered McKinzie. A man who wore the mantle of honor and authority as naturally as most men wore their own skins.

Yancey Hamilton, once Belle Terre's bad boy and now a man with mysterious and powerful associations—associations that prompted Jefferson's call for his help—waited a little distance away. Ethan Garrett, except for Simon the most unexpected element in this mix of different and unique men, stood by Yancey. Yet, on second thought, Ethan—who was the brother of Jefferson's own brother's wife and a man given to protracted, unexplained absences—fit perfectly in this mix of competent, enigmatic men. Men, Jefferson knew in a glance, for whom danger was a way of life. And honor their reason for being.

"Quite a welcoming committee," he observed. "Because of the Argentine connection?"

"Is that a question?" Rick asked.

"An observation, Rick."

"That's what I thought. You know everybody?"

Jefferson's gaze returned to the impressive gathering. "Except for Mr. McKinzie, I thought I did. Now I'm not so sure."

Rick rose from his seat. "They're still the men you knew, but you're about to see another side of all of us. The side Simon McKinzie saw when he recruited us for The Black Watch."

* * *

"Gentlemen." Simon McKinzie addressed the men gathered in the office of his mountain retreat. A place where The Black Watch came only rarely. Even more rarely, civilians, as he considered those not a part of the clandestine government organization that he had formed by order of a past president, and had solely controlled in the many years since. "Summing up. According to his ongoing dossier, in aspiring to become the next drug czar of the world, Vicente Menendez was determined to buy certain connections in Argentina as an alternate route of distribution through virgin territory. He chose an older man, thinking he would be more vulnerable. But, Menendez didn't reckon with the integrity and iron will of Paulo Rei. Nor was he prepared for a woman as spectacularly beautiful and accomplished as Rei's wife.

"Señora Rei would be remembered by all of you as Merrie Alexandre. To all but Jefferson. To whom, I'm told, she has always been Marissa Claire, her true, given name. Then, there's Rick, of course, who hasn't met the charming lady. A condition we should rectify, hopefully and soon. Any questions, thus far?"

No one spoke and Simon continued. "Menendez assumed, for a price, not only would Rei's honor be for sale, so would his young wife. We suspect that in underestimating his prey, Menendez revealed more of his operation than was prudent. Before he had understood Rei was a man whose honor was priceless, as was his wife's loyalty. After the brief suspicion of a bomb, we have reason to believe that fearing exposure and infuriated by Señora Rei's rejection, Menendez ordered their plane shot down over the sea.

"This was purely speculation based on the suspicions of an informant. Until Jefferson called Jericho, we had no reason to think Marissa Rei was alive. Even if we had, we wouldn't have known where to look for her. Now we do.

Because Jefferson recognized the need for secrecy, we just might succeed.''

"So, we're going after her." Playing devil's advocate, Rick Cahill locked stares with Simon. "Why?"

"Because she's an American citizen, born in America of an American mother. Because Menendez is also an American, one who destroys lives for profit. Because I want him." A cold stare turned colder. "Does that answer the question?"

Without waiting for a response, Simon looked at his men. Each of whom possessed unique talents, unique abilities, and infinite loyalty. "So we go?"

"We go." Rick spoke first. A surprise to no one, including Jefferson, who had learned many surprising things this day.

The land was rugged and breathtaking and vast. The sturdy horse he'd been provided was an excellent mount. The trail he rode was not difficult if ridden with concentration and caution. At his back, but beyond sight, lay the Alexandres's Argentine *estancia,* an oasis in the heart of a plain. Ahead, the Patagonian Alps, a part of the continent-spanning Andes, sprawled like sleeping giants. That the woman who was his guide knew the land and its irregularities was immediately apparent. Jefferson's only chore was to follow and keep Simon's timetable.

So, ever cognizant of the hour, he followed and worried about what he would find at their destination. And what would happen to the good people who had helped Marissa when she and he, and Simon's men of The Black Watch were gone.

Go with caution to the Alexandre estancia, to Marta Elia, wife of the foreman. Horses and a guide will be provided. The rest we leave to you.

The scant message that brought him here was a brand in

his mind. One he would never forget. As he would never forget Marta Elia and her husband Juan. Marissa's allies who offered secret sanctuary to a friend with no concern for the trouble they might bring down on themselves.

"If Menendez finds out...if he finds them..." Jefferson didn't want to think of it. Instead he fixed his gaze on Marta's back, and on little Alejandro, her three-year-old son, who clung like a limpet to her waist. When she'd ridden into the copse of stunted trees where she'd directed him to wait, he hadn't expected she would be his guide, nor that she would bring the child.

At first, given the obvious need for both speed and secrecy, he was disturbed by the boy's presence. But he needn't have been. Alejandro had ridden for hours beneath the blazing sun and had never complained. As the terrain gave way to a series of small rocky hillocks to climb and descend, the trail required more attention. But not so much that Jefferson didn't wonder how it would be to have such a son. Or perhaps a daughter.

He would have been startled at a thought so foreign to what he expected his life to be, if Marta hadn't slowed her horse and announced quietly, "We are here, *señor.*"

The plain was still and quiet but for the hum of the ever-blowing wind. Nothing moved in the empty expanse, and for all the hours of their ride, the mountains seemed no closer. The stark beauty Jefferson had found in the land was only cruel and harsh as fear closed about his heart like an icy fist.

Had Marta made a mistake? Was this not the rendezvous? Or had something gone wrong? Menendez?

"Marissa." A shudder shook Jefferson's lean, hard frame. Her name was a strangled whisper caught in the wind. And not even the blaze of the sun could warm him.

Then the bulky figure of a man was rising from an overgrown outcrop of stone where there should be none. He did not wear the celebrated ballooning pants of the gaucho. But his shaggy, dark hair just visible beneath his flat brimmed hat, his handsome features and demeanor left little doubt that he was one of the renowned horsemen of the Argentine pampas.

He carried no weapons but the tools of his work. Yet Jefferson didn't question that he was a man who would protect what was his, or that his name was Juan. A shattered breath later, Marissa stepped from the curtain of scraggly vegetation that rimmed the stones, and out of Juan Elia's shadow.

"I'm here, Jefferson." Her voice was music.

As he heard her, Jefferson's labored breath caught in his lungs. His mouth went dry, even as his heart lurched in an uneven rhythm. A woman so different from the woman he remembered, but still so beautiful, waited beneath his startled stare.

Her long brown hair had been cut shorter. No scarf held the sleek, sophisticated mane in check as it brushed the line of her shoulders. Beneath the low-tipped brim of a hat similar to that of her companion's, her face was angular and too thin, revealing bone structure that promised lasting beauty in happiness or grief, old or young. Her eyes were shadowed and veiled as she held his gaze.

On a glance he had seen that she was too slender, too worn by her ordeal. Trousers of dark leather clung to her long legs and brushed the toes of her boots, making a tall woman seem taller, a slender woman, more slender. A lighter vest hung open over a soft shirt and brushed the belt buckled at her waist.

Marissa, dressed as he'd seen her hundreds of times. As strong as he knew she would be. Resting an unsteady hand on the pommel of his saddle, vaguely aware that Marta, Juan, and even Alejandro watched him, and waited, he asked, "Are you all right?"

Her eyelids swept down, shielding her eyes from his. Her lashes brushed the line of her cheekbone. But neither they nor the shadow of her hat could hide the toll of tragedy.

Then, as a strong woman rediscovered her faltering stamina, her lashes swept up. As her dark gaze met his again, her somber lips tilted in a wavering smile. "I will be," she said in barely more than a whisper. "Now that you're here."

Now that you're here. The words he didn't know he'd waited for, spoken in the voice of the cultured woman. But with the wistfulness of the girl he'd first loved.

In a fluid dismount, Jefferson was out of the saddle and on the ground and Marissa was in his arms. "You're safe now, sweetheart," he promised against her hair as her hat went spinning in the wind and the dust.

Burrowing deeper into his embrace, her forehead against his shoulder, Marissa breathed in the familiar scent of him and reveled in his gentle touch. The scent she'd never forgotten. The touch that filled her dreams. "I was afraid you might not care. That you wouldn't come."

Moving her away only a little, a knuckle beneath her chin lifted her face and her gaze to his. "I promised, Marissa. Remember? If ever you need me…"

"I'll come for you," she finished for him as he intended she should. "And now you have. I should never have doubted a promise made by such a special friend. No matter how long ago." Her laugh was low, a trembling sound, and there were tears on her cheeks. "First Juan and Marta, and now you, Jefferson. Friends risking your lives for mine. It's more than I deserve. You're all so much more than I deserve."

"No." Jefferson gathered her back to him, to hide the tears he couldn't bear to see. "Never more than that."

As he held Marissa, Jefferson was aware that Juan and Marta had moved away. Stealing rare moments for themselves even as they were giving reunited friends time alone. But only a little time, for in the distance he heard the rhythmic throb of a helicopter. The percussions of the blades grew closer and louder each passing minute. Though he didn't want to let her go, there were duties to attend. Decisions to be made.

Releasing Marissa, but taking her hand, he went with her to Juan and Marta as they stood by the mass of stones. It was then Jefferson realized that rather than random rubble, they were part of the ruins of a structure. A home once, perhaps. One, he suspected, that served again as shelter.

Shelter for Marissa in the weeks since the crash of Paulo Rei's plane. But what shelter would there be for this small family? Who would be their allies? If danger threatened, how could those who would repay their kindness help? Jefferson knew the collective answer to his question. Simon and the men and women of The Black Watch would offer and insure sanctuary for the Elias as the Elias offered sanctuary to Marissa. So would Jefferson Cade.

Addressing Juan and Marta, he spoke into the escalating cacophony. "The men for whom we wait are coming. There will be room in the helicopter for both of you and your son. It won't be safe here if it's discovered Marissa wasn't on the plane and that you helped her.

"If you come with us, Simon assures safe passage into our country. With that, I promise a home and work for Juan with my brothers in the southeast. Or, if he chooses, with me in the west. Above all, we pledge you will be safe."

Juan had turned to face Jefferson and Marissa. With Alejandro in his arms, his eyes dwelt on the face of the young woman he had known all her life. "Marta and I understand the danger. We have from the first."

"Then you know it's impossible for you to stay." Jefferson met a dark gaze that took his measure.

"Do you understand the danger if we go, Señor Cade?" Juan countered, as he put his son down to play.

"You're afraid that if you and Marta and Alejandro disappear there will be an investigation. Possibly raising suspicions that could lead to speculations about me." Marissa's hand grew taut in Jefferson's as she saw beyond grief and guilt to the magnitude of what her friends had risked to help her.

"Any investigation will bring outsiders to the *estancia, querida.* People who will question, perhaps too skillfully. And someone will remember you were here, helping Marta with Alejandro's illness when it was thought you were on the plane. The time and place and circumstances will be investigated, and someone will realize the value of what he or she knows." Leaving the rest of his warning unsaid, Juan drew a harsh breath.

"Menendez has already proven his influence and his power. Someone will talk. For money, or in pain. Then he will search for you." The gaucho's darkly weathered face was grim. "The rotten threads of his ugly empire reach far and wide. His thugs know how to make the most unwilling speak. Wherever you are he will find you. And if he cannot take you, he will kill you, Rissa."

"That's the chance I prefer. The chance I would gladly take. Looking over my shoulder, waiting for Menendez would be easier than living in fear of what could happen to you and Marta, and to Alejandro." Marissa looked from Juan to Marta, to Alejandro who played quietly in the dust. "He's the child I couldn't have, I won't risk losing him."

"This is our country." Juan was adamant. "The *estancia* has been my home. If we stay, no suspicions will be aroused. The only newcomers will be those who inherit what your father left. We will be as safe here as anywhere, once you're gone."

"You don't think someone might remember, as you say,

and talk to the new owners?'' Jefferson drew Marissa back to him. With his arm resting across her shoulder, he discovered the brush of the tips of her hair against his wrist had the power to tantalize, even in times of crisis.

''We are an isolated people, caring little for what happens in the world beyond the plain. The news of the crash and the suspicion of a bomb came first to me. Marissa was already in hiding before I spoke of the deaths to anyone. For all those of the *estancia* know, she had gone to join her family on the plane.

''Later, on the occasion of my visits here, Marta made sensible, believable explanations.'' Juan's look met Jefferson's, daring him to doubt Marta. ''As she convinced the curious you were an American journalist seeking a story, Señor Cade.''

''It's too flimsy, Juan. You can't trust that no one will question the timing.'' It was naive of the gaucho to believe he could protect Marissa so easily. But Jefferson realized he couldn't convince this most stubborn man of it. A man who didn't want to uproot his family and turn his back on the only way of life he'd ever known any less than he wanted to see Marissa hurt.

Recognizing that as a stranger he couldn't sway this stalwart and uncompromising man, Jefferson bowed out of the argument, hoping Marissa might succeed where he could not. With a subtle pressure on the curve of her shoulder, he relinquished the debate to her.

Marissa stood silently as she considered what her lifelong friend and protector must be feeling. When she spoke, her voice was steady, her tone low. ''Then you've decided, and nothing can sway you. You won't go.''

''No, *querida*.'' Juan's arms were crossed over his chest, his feet planted firmly. As firmly as his resolve.

''What about Marta?'' Marissa tried one last ploy.

''Marta wants what I want, as always.''

Marissa only nodded. She'd always known Juan and Marta shared a love unlike any she'd ever known. That they seemed to feel the same and think alike on almost every issue.

Almost. Moving beyond Jefferson's touch, Marissa stepped closer to Juan. She was tall, he was taller. Her head tipped back, dark eyes held his. "Then I stay, too."

"No!" Jefferson objected. "You don't know what you're saying." He would have brought her back to him, back into his arms, but with a raised hand, she warded him off.

"I know very well what I'm saying. I'm staying here to protect my friends as they protected me. And to watch Alejandro grow up. If that means going to Menendez, then I will." Turning to him, she smiled a regretful smile. "I'm sorry, Jefferson. More than you can know." Her voice faded and faltered.

She looked away. At the ground, at the sky, anywhere but at Jefferson. Then, with her composure restored, she continued. "If I could change what Menendez has done, I would. But I can't, any more than I can leave the people who've done so much for me, and mean so much to me, to suffer the consequence of my defection."

"You're going to strike a bargain with Menendez?" It was Juan who was first to make sense of her hushed words.

She wouldn't deny what couldn't be denied. "If I can."

"Marissa, selling her body and soul again, for someone else." Jefferson's tone was bleak and bitterly mocking.

"Ask yourself what you would do, Jefferson." She looked from one man to another. "And you, Juan, would you not make a bargain with the devil to save someone you love?"

Jefferson had no answer. None except that he would do what he had to for Marissa. As the helicopter came closer, he made his decision. "It's settled then. If one stays, we all stay."

"You're wrong." Marta, who had only listened, lifted her son from the ground to settle him against her breasts. "My husband thinks with his heart, not his head. We go. All of us."

Then she addressed Juan. "We have no one here. You have no family. I have none. We don't know who will be the new owner, or if we will be happy. And if someone wants to talk about Marissa and the plane, they will whether we're here or not. This is a chance for Alejandro. One we must take."

Juan said nothing as his look turned to his son whose eyes were droopy with fatigue. Finally his dark gaze met Marta's. "You're sure, my love?"

Marta was steadfast and unwavering. "I'm sure."

Her answer was almost lost in the drone of the helicopter making its landing approach. A much larger craft than the two Jefferson had traveled in days ago. One meant to accommodate more than two added passengers.

"Come." Catching the reins of Marta's horse, Juan beckoned to him. "We must unsaddle the horses and set them free."

As Marissa went to calm her mount and Juan's, already unsaddled and ground tied in a cluster of misshapen, windpruned trees, Jefferson stripped both saddle and blanket from his mount. Then, bridle in hand, he waited while Juan led the other three horses to his.

In a shout Jefferson said, "We shouldn't leave anything behind. I don't know what suspicions it might raise if the saddles and bridles were found here. Or even if it would matter at all. But it would be best if no one had reason to suspect this land had been a recent campsite of any sort."

"Then what do you propose?" Juan asked.

"That we take everything. Saddles, bridles, blankets. Anything connected to the Alexandre *estancia*."

The chance of more conversation was swept away in a lowering clamor. With a grim flash of teeth, Juan slipped the bridle from his mount and Marta's and set them free. Jefferson was only a second behind with his horse and Marissa's. The animals might return to their home pastures, or roam the plains. But grass and water would be plentiful wherever they wandered.

While the men had released the tethered horses, Marta and Marissa had cleared the area. Leaving no trace of the weeks she'd spent in the tumbled ruins that were once a home.

The helicopter hovered and waited. Close enough that Jefferson could see Rick Cahill was at the controls, as he'd expected. Yancey Hamilton and Ethan Garrett were standing guard, armed and ready. A testimony of Simon's grave concern.

The touchdown was to be brief. Only long enough to take on passengers and gear. With a hand from Yancey, Marissa, Alejandro and Marta were boarded, while Ethan took the saddles and other paraphernalia. Next was Juan, and finally Jefferson.

"Ready?" Rick called above revving engines.

Giving a thumbs-up, Jefferson agreed. "Take her up."

Flashing a smile, Rick complied. As the nearly fully loaded chopper lifted off, the windstorm of the blades swept the plain clean of any footprint or proof that either man or woman or child had ever been there.

Jefferson looked across the craft at Juan and Marta, and Alejandro. A silent child, as brave as his parents.

As he brushed a hand over dry, burning eyes, the last person he saw was Marissa. With a tired sigh, he smiled.

If ever you need me…

A promise kept.

Three

Debriefing.

A strange word for a peaceful valley. But no more strange than the way this began. No more strange than now.

After another journey, a long, convoluted flight from the Argentine plain, and a restless night spent in Simon McKinzie's retreat, Jefferson stood at the edge of a jagged precipice beneath a gnarled evergreen. The valley below was calm, with no hint of troubles and danger that had been dealt with, or the threat of more to come. For hours he had studied this bastion. Because of what he'd seen, he felt no concern as Marissa walked the lakeshore. Or that Alejandro played with the youngest of the Canfield boys and their half-grown Doberman pups under the watchful eye of Raven Canfield. Simon's beloved goddaughter, mother of the Canfield children.

Jefferson's first time in the valley had been too short, too intense to allow time for more than business. He'd been too intent on the letter, and the message encoded within the newspaper article, to be observant of more than obvious facets of the land. He could think of little beyond the simplistic marking of partial words. Marks readily apparent, but only to one keenly interested in every aspect of the message. Only to one who understood the handwritten recollection of a promise, and realized the mistake in the news report. One who knew there must be more.

In retrospect and better informed, Jefferson recognized the frightening risk the letter represented. He understood the gamble that in the right hands the message would be discovered. In the wrong, tossed away in disinterest. A desperate gamble. Thank God, one that had worked in all its simplicity.

Chance. Much had been based on that happenstance and the thread of good fortune woven into tragedy. Chance, good fortune, good friends. But it wasn't over yet. Jefferson knew it would never be as long as Menendez and his minions walked the earth. Ruthless, corrupt, worshiping power and wealth.

Had Marissa known how prophetic her words were when she spoke of looking over her shoulder? he wondered in one moment. The next, he realized that she knew better than anyone. In a rush of anger for all she'd lost and endured, there was passion. The thrill of awareness that began like a whisper, touching his heart, his mind, his body. Until every sense was held in thrall, remembering a look, a smile, the heat of her hand in his. Until his arms ached to hold her, and his mouth hungered for her kiss. Until he wanted to lay the world at her feet, a better, safer place.

For want of a better world, he would make their part of it the best he could. If she must look over her shoulder…
"I'll be looking, too," he promised. "For as long as it takes."

As he spoke, his attention moved over the valley. The

safest of places with a gathering of men who risked their lives for Marissa and her friends. Who would again, if they must.

This, he'd discovered, was the other side of the men he knew. Men with qualities and strengths Simon recognized and drew to him. As the first McKinzies recognized the strengths of the valley and made it their home. A land nearly as impregnable as it was beautiful. A haven for Simon. With David Canfield, the first recruit of The Black Watch, to guard it in his absence.

"Canfield." Jefferson considered the quiet, rugged man. Retired with honor and always the standard for all who followed in his footsteps. Big footsteps but, he'd discovered, with big men filling them. Thoughts of Canfield led naturally to Raven. His lovely, dark-haired wife, whose heart was as big as any footstep. A heart that embraced Marissa, the Elias, and especially Alejandro, welcoming them into her home.

Jefferson smiled as he thought of life spent in the McKinzies's valley. For with Simon, he was learning the unexpected was the norm. But if the gallant lady who had lived most of her life with the McKinzies was perturbed by helicopters or strange men and women arriving at her doorstep, it hadn't shown by so much as a flutter of her long, dark lashes.

Shortly, the helicopter should return with the last member of The Watch Simon had summoned. Then they would get on with the rest of their plans, and their lives. Until then, Jefferson worked off the restlessness that kept him from sleeping, eating and being congenial company, by exploring the valley. And, he admitted paying homage to truth, guarding Marissa.

"What are you thinking?" he wondered from his distant watchtower as she walked along the shore lost in another world. Once she would have reveled in the scent of Raven's wildflower garden. Now she passed it by without a glance. An eagle's cry echoed above the valley. In another time she would have searched the sky for a glimpse of it. Now she didn't seem to hear.

He'd expected a tumult of emotions now that her circumstances had changed. Grief and, in part, the guilt Juan had addressed. But this emotion was more powerful and much deeper. Given this silent withdrawal, it was something she plainly intended to deal with alone. Just as plainly, whatever it was that weighed so heavily on her mind and her heart, it was consuming her.

"What is it, Marissa? What hurts you so, and how can I help?" Even as his own words fell into the silence hovering far above the valley floor, he knew there was little he could do. Little but deny his desire, forget the ache in his heart and body, and watch from afar. As now, he would watch, he would keep her safe, he would wait. Then, one day—if that one day could ever come—he would speak to her with his heart, not his voice.

A trill of laughter caught by a breeze drew his attention to the boys. The Canfield boy, whose name was Dare, was several years older than Alejandro, but in their game and on this clear, sunny day, age didn't seem to matter. On the fading note of laughter, Jefferson heard the sound he was expecting. A sound that had become more than familiar in a matter of days.

Time to go. Time to weigh issues and make decisions. Another skilled and unique agent had arrived. It was Yancey who had flown the chopper out of the valley before dawn. With instincts and skill rivaling Rick Cahill.

Jefferson wasn't surprised by this newly revealed accomplishment of a lifelong friend from Belle Terre. He'd decided, short of treason and conduct unbecoming a gentleman, nothing of Simon McKinzie or his Black Watch would surprise him.

Now, as he left the precipice and moved down the mountain, he wondered who would come and go in Simon's scheme of operations. His part as initial contact done, Jericho had returned to his duties as sheriff of Belle Terre. The new man, or woman, would take Simon's plan to the next step. Rather than speculate who that person might be, Jefferson wondered if Yancey's flight was as convoluted as his had been with Rick.

"Bet on it, Cade. With safety and stealth the order of the day, how else would the leader of The Watch have it?"

Though he made the trip down at a rapid pace, by the time he reached the valley floor, Yancey Hamilton had set the chopper down and cut the engine. It was Billy Blackhawk, who unfolded his massive body from the "duck and run" beyond spinning blades.

There was no time for surprise as Blackhawk's hand enveloped his. "Jeff." Half Apache and a match for Jericho in size, the sheriff of Silverton said sincerely, "Glad you made it."

"You, too," Jefferson drawled in return. "And just when I thought I couldn't be surprised."

Blackhawk grinned. "Just wait, there will be more."

"Yep." Yancey flung an arm around Jefferson's shoulder. "Never doubt it. Simon's full of tricks."

Poker-faced, Jefferson muttered, "Not just Simon."

By unspoken consensus, along with Juan and Marta, the men who regathered in Simon's office left the two seats closest to Simon's desk for Marissa and Jefferson. As he held her chair, she looked only at his hands, never at his face. Certainly never his eyes. As she caught her lower lip briefly between her teeth in a familiar gesture he hadn't seen in so long, he feared she would flee. Not from the office, not from the gathering, but from him. Instead, after a tense interval, she took the seat he offered with a husky "Thank you, Jefferson."

While Jefferson took his seat beside and a bit in back of Marissa, Simon spoke. "Ladies." As he turned to Marissa, then Marta, eyes that could freeze an antagonist with a single glance, were warm, even smiling. "I commend you.

"And you, gentlemen." Not so warm, not so smiling, he spoke to his chosen. And to Jefferson and Juan. "From the beginning you've made wise, intuitive choices." A massive hand lifted, blunt-tipped fingers splayed. "Beginning with Señor Elia's recognition that Señora Rei should be shielded from public notice until the truth of the crash was determined."

One finger folded into Simon's palm.

"Then Señora Rei, or if I may, Marissa?" Simon paused, all eyes turned to her. Including Jefferson's, and he was struck by her regal posture, the utter control with which she faced Simon. A veneer that had slipped on the plain, firmly in place again.

As she neither blushed, nor faltered, but nodded with a subtle smile, Jefferson realized Marissa Rei was two women in one. The courageous woman who refused to leave her friends to face the unknown in her stead. And, as now, the woman who had learned to hide her emotions— whether pain, grief, or concern—with cool control and uncompromising grace.

"Marissa, then," Simon agreed and returned to his habitual enumeration with his hand still raised. "Second was Marissa's plan to have her messages to Jefferson pass through the hands of several trusted college friends."

A second finger folded into a broad palm, but Jefferson didn't notice. His attention was riveted on Marissa. A Marissa he was seeing for the first time. Understanding for the first time. Yet one who had been there all the while.

She was the woman of strength who was part of the

young daredevil—a girl sent away from her own country, who made the new country home. The woman of courage who was part of the horsewoman who challenged any horse however frenzied and tamed it. She was the compassionate woman who was part of the huntress who was never ashamed of a heart too tender to harm any creature. She was the devoted woman in the daughter who had sacrificed, and would sacrifice, her own life and love for family and friends.

She was the daredevil, the horsewoman, the huntress, the daughter. And the woman they had made of her had been his friend.

Just once, she'd been his lover. With his brilliant gaze never leaving her, not caring who might see and read what was in his face, he vowed she would be again.

"That's the lot." Simon finished his enumerated praise with the last point made, the last finger fisted. A known gesture to longtime associates. It would become familiar to the rest. "Which brings us to the present and where we go from here.

"Marissa, Juan, Marta, it's most important you stay hidden for a while. How long, I can't say. But we need time to prove our suspicions and to corner Menendez. Until we do…"

Marissa clasped her hands tightly in her lap. "I understand. I'm sure we all do."

"Belle Terre, or the horse farms and plantations nearby are out of the question. You could be recognized. Unless there's another suggestion, I'm offering my home here." With a look at David Canfield, who stood by the door, Simon continued, "David will be here to serve as your bodyguard, along with Juan. More guards will be posted at points along the route into the—

"Jefferson," Simon interrupted himself. "You have a problem with this? I assume that's what the scowl means."

"No problem. Just that this isn't what I expected. I thought...I assumed Marissa would go to the Broken Spur with me. It's isolated, but surrounded by land that's patrolled. No one in the country would know her. Recognition would be a long shot."

"Good!" Simon exclaimed. "I hoped you would volunteer. In fact, it was for that reason I asked Billy to join us. Now the choice is up to Marissa and to Juan and Marta. But before you make your decision, I'll let Billy tell you what protections he can offer and will have in place."

Billy Blackhawk walked to a bare wall. Pulling down a map from a cornice, he began to explain. "Isolation and anonymity. This valley and the canyon offer both. The difference is space and manpower. Because Sandy Gannon keeps a close eye on Jake Benedict's empire, riders for the brand patrol this area constantly. An added man or two here, here, here—" a tanned finger tapped strategic corners of the map "—shouldn't cause suspicion.

"Added to that, Jake just acquired a small operation here." Another tap on the map, then with a slow sweep of his arm, Billy indicated a straight line intersecting the borders of both a thin strip of existing Benedict land, and the Broken Spur. "As the crow flies, the ride would be no more than an hour at an easy pace. Sandy has sent out word that he's looking for a tenant who knows cattle and horses and can tend the ranch and the land."

Billy looked then at Juan and Marta. "I've spoken to Sandy, the job's yours, Elia, if you want it." Big hands, strong and graceful at once, made a gesture of finality. "That's it. All that's left is the decision."

In the hours and days since Jefferson had come for her as he promised, Marissa had retreated within herself, dealing with a storm of grief and guilt, and unexpected emotions. She hadn't thought beyond each minute. She hadn't considered that life couldn't go on exactly as it was. "It didn't occur to me, I didn't think—'' Breaking off, she shook her head, shedding her lethargy. "In different circumstances I would prefer the valley. But that could bring danger to Raven's children. To be honest, I don't consider the Broken Spur a suitable choice either. But if there's nowhere else then..."

Lifting a weary shoulder, she said hoarsely, "I'm sorry, I'm not making sense. I think I must defer to those of you with better knowledge of the situation."

"Jefferson?" Simon laid the decision on the table.

Marissa had made it clear she didn't want the Broken Spur. But Jefferson had no intention of letting a third option crop up. "I'm scheduled to manage the ranch for at least another year. It's a two-man operation, with one man in residence, I would appreciate having an expert horse trainer like Marissa on the premises."

"In other words, you're offering the pretty lady a job," Yancey drawled in his best Southern accent.

"Why not?" Jefferson grinned. "She's a good hand."

Marissa looked from Jefferson to the Elias. "Juan?"

Juan, in turn, looked at his wife, who nodded. Then his solemn gaze returned to Marissa. "We would choose the ranch Señor Gannon offered. Alejandro would like it if you were close."

Marissa drew a long, considering breath, though there was nothing to consider. This was an opportunity such as Juan never could have expected in his own country. But if she didn't go to the Broken Spur, he wouldn't take it. She couldn't let a sudden deluge of grief and guilt deny these good people who had denied her nothing. Not even their lives.

"Then it's settled," she said in a voice that hid her fears for herself and for Jefferson in the days to come. "We go to the Broken Spur, and to Jake Benedict's new land."

* * *

The meeting dispersed shortly after Marissa's decision. Simon had made it clear he applauded her choice. And for the record, Yancey, a very silent Ethan, and Rick agreed. Billy Blackhawk had been clear on his choice from the first.

The three who had been most actively and dangerously involved stood in a group on the porch. They each turned from the view of the lake at moonrise as Marissa approached them. "Gentlemen." Her greeting was quiet. As each turned to her, with a gesture, a smile, or a nod, she addressed them separately. "Rick, Ethan, and Yancey, I can't begin to thank you for what you've done and what you've risked for my friends and for me."

When they would have protested, claiming it as all in a day's work, a day when nothing really unfortunate happened, she would have none of it. "The risk was there, a risk that could have meant your life, yet you took it willingly for people who were little more than strangers."

"Not quite, sweet Merrie," Yancey reminded her. "If I hadn't helped, half of Belle Terre and all the Cade brothers would have lifted my scalp. If they found it out."

An in-law of the Cades, of sorts, by way of his sister's marriage into the family, Ethan chuckled. "Yancey has that right. Rick isn't that familiar with Belle Terre or he would understand, as I came to understand in a short time, that the male half of the population of that most illustrious Southern city was head over boot heels in love with Merrie Alexandre. If we'd let anything happen to you, we would have that posse to face."

"I second that," Jefferson said from the shadows beyond the small circle of uniquely trained and accomplished men. Head over boot heels was an apt description of himself as well. And the years of separation hadn't changed what he felt.

Marissa turned to him, her expression calm, but with something unfathomable in her eyes. "Jefferson, I didn't see you there." She was flustered, unsettled. But, as quickly, she regained the monumental poise he'd just witnessed in the meeting. "I should be thanking you as much as these gentlemen. Perhaps more, for setting in motion the chain of events that brought Juan, Marta, and Alejandro to safety with me."

"Would you have me do otherwise, Marissa?" Jefferson asked, speaking as calmly and as quietly as she had spoken. But any who knew him would have heard the thread of tension, the taunting, questioning satire. "When you sent the letter, did you for one minute think I could *not* do what I did?"

He left unsaid that for him four years was an eternity in days, hours, weeks and months. But even an eternity couldn't erase his memories or ease his heart. Just as her strange attitude might hurt, yet still altered nothing. "I don't want your gratitude, Marissa. In fact, gratitude is the last thing I want."

His face was grim as he turned away. He would have left her then in the company of Simon's men, but Billy Blackhawk loomed before him with Simon only a step away. Their private discussion finished, both had come to join the gathering on the porch. The final plans concerning Marissa and the Elias had been resolved before the meeting adjourned, leaving time for pleasantries.

Jefferson was no more in the mood for pleasantries than for gratitude. He needed space, solitude. Time to organize his thoughts, to gather the willpower to curb his desire and his need for Marissa. Before, he hadn't thought past the message or considered the future. All he could think was that she was in trouble and she needed him. Worrying about how he would fit in to her life and she in his, hadn't been an option.

Neither was hurting her, but he had. Damning himself for flinging her gratitude back in her face, he stood in the gathering twilight, with twining currents of the heated air of the day and the cool of the night swirling about him. Of all the scents woven among them, it was her scent that caressed his skin. Her scent he breathed. Of all the looks that glanced at him, then looked away, it was her somber questioning look he saw.

He couldn't bear another minute. As conversation dwindled to a halt, he addressed Simon and Billy. "If there's nothing more to discuss that's pertinent to our plans, I'd like to take a walk by the lake before turning in."

He didn't wait for an answer. With a tilt of his bare head, he left the porch and crossed the stepping stones that led to the lake. At his back the buzz of conversation began again, before him there was the tranquil mountain lake.

Tranquillity that escaped him as he strolled the worn path. Laughter drifted over the water, a moment of returned camaraderie in the wake of tension. Farther along as drooping limbs of hemlock and pine surrounded him, he heard the pad of a footstep and the scrape of a claw against stone behind him.

Turning, he recognized the female Doberman, only because she was the smaller dog. "Jazz." Curling his hand around her cropped ears in a gesture the dog obviously enjoyed, he asked, "What are you doing out here alone?"

"Jazz isn't alone, Jefferson." Marissa skirted the limb of a hemlock. "She came with me." Pausing, gathering her courage she asked, "Would you mind if we walk with you?"

Jefferson hesitated only a half second. "Of course not." Normally he would have taken a woman's arm, even her hand, but tonight with Marissa, he simply walked in silence by her side. A quarter of the way around the natural lake fed by a waterfall and artesian springs, beyond the spill of light from the cabins, she stopped him with a light touch at his wrist.

When he halted she was waiting for his attention. "I'm sorry, Jefferson. I shouldn't have called on you. But I thought that after the years, I…we…" Curious at the sudden, faltering silence, Jazz nuzzled her hand. The hand that had touched him. Finally she continued. "I shouldn't have dragged you into this."

"Who else would you ask, Marissa?" Her hair was silvered by moonlight. She was light and darkness with eyes like midnight. And he was cold and cruel. Something he never believed he could be to any woman. Especially Marissa.

Something he wouldn't be. Certainly not to Marissa. Touching her face, brushing a wayward strand of dark silk from her cheek he tucked it behind her ear. "You were right to reach out to me. I didn't know how right until I met Simon, and his men. I'm sure there were others who would have tried. College friends, even others in Argentina. But would they have had Simon's resources, or men like Yancey and Rick and Ethan? Could they have offered a valley such as this, or a friend like Raven?"

"Or like you," she added softly.

"My part in this?" A small gesture encompassed the valley, the towering mountains, the security. And most of all, though it was hidden by the foliage of trees and laurel and rhododendron, Simon's home and the men who gathered there. "Purely the luck of a telephone call. I had no idea how to begin, or who to contact, so I called Jericho and asked for Yancey.

"I knew from past situations that he had mysterious and powerful connections. Since he can be anywhere in the world at any given time, I knew that if anyone could find him, it would be Jericho. That call was the beginner's luck of this."

A shrug of shoulders that had grown heavier and stronger through the years dismissed his part in her deliverance.

"The rest, God willing, is history. Tomorrow the future begins."

Marissa stared at him. She was taller than average, but still looked up at him. His face, tilted down, was in shadow. But in the silvered gold of the rising moon, his rough clothes were no longer the sensible jeans and boots of a horseman, but the mantle of a knight's armor. Though the once turquoise-banded mane was cut short and silver that owed nothing to moonlight dusted the darkened blond of his hair, he was still the Prince Charming she had thought she would never find in the swamp.

He would be that modern-day prince, that kind knight. In the swamp, on the plain, in a valley or a desert, in her heart. For that was the sort of man he was. The man he would always be.

"Tomorrow," she whispered, and clenched her hands to keep from touching him again.

Hearing the unsteady note in her voice, Jefferson framed her face with caressing fingers, gently raising her gaze to his. "Don't be afraid, Marissa. We'll do all right together at the ranch. Nothing will hurt you there." Then, remembering his curt words on Simon's porch, he murmured, "Nor will I."

"I'm not afraid, Jefferson. Not anymore. And never of you." As he looked down at her, his face was still veiled in darkness, but she knew it would reflect the tenderness in his touch. A touch that made her want to tilt her lips into his palm, to trace the gentle power there with her kiss.

Want that turned to searing pain, and to shattering guilt, as she remembered another kind and gentle man. *Paulo.*

"I should go." Backing away, one hand reaching out to caress the sleek and elegant head of the Doberman, she looked at the mountains that were only black and deep purple shapes lying beneath a darkening sky. She looked at the bright glitter of the lake as it gave back the light of the moon in countless ripples. She drew a deep breath, savoring the scent of honeysuckle and evergreen. Blended with it, the crisp, clean scent of sunshine and fresh mountain air that lingered on Jefferson.

For this moment she could almost imagine a different world where grief and guilt could never dishonor love.

"Marissa?"

She heard his concern, and only then realized that she was staring at him. "It's nothing." She evaded the truth and added the sin of lying by omission to her long list of guilt. "Tomorrow will be a long and busy day. I'll leave you to your walk and your thoughts." She meant to go, to flee from the churn of her emotions. But her conscience wouldn't let her. "I am sorry for what I've done to your life. For the danger I've put you in.

"Perhaps there were others I could have called on or turned to. But the truth is, I didn't consider anyone else. Without regard to what helping me would mean, or how it would disrupt your life, I thought only of you." Her head bowed, she stared at the ground, but saw Jefferson as he'd been that last day in the tree house. Tall, handsome, a golden man with eyes like sapphires. Her best friend, her gentle teacher, a tender lover. The man she couldn't forget.

Her head came up, she looked into the shadow of his face. "I wanted you, Jefferson."

Not sure how to interpret her words, Jefferson stood like carved darkness as he watched her walk away. "Don't be a fool, Cade," he muttered. "Don't read into this what you want it to be."

He was her trusted friend. It was natural that she would want him...to keep a promise.

A long while later, Jefferson retraced his steps, returning to the clearing. Simon's house still blazed with lights. The Canfields's was dark. He hoped that meant Marissa slept. She would need her rest for the journey tomorrow.

"Jefferson." Stepping from the gloom of a copse of pines, Raven fell into step beside him. The clasp of her hand at his elbow brought him to a halt. "Would you listen to someone who understands what Marissa is facing and has felt as she feels now?"

He knew from Yancey that Raven had lost her family as horrendously as Marissa had, but at a much younger age. Remembered hurt was there now in the reflected light of Simon's windows. "If that someone were you, Raven, I would listen to anything."

A nod acknowledged she understood he knew her history. Her smile was bittersweet. "Go carefully. Be as patient as Jericho says you can be. Treat each day as a separate accomplishment. Don't rush her, but don't let her heap guilt on herself.

"Most of all remember, through no fault of yours, you're a part of her guilt. If she lashes out or turns away from you, it will be for what you represent, not you. Wait for her then."

"What guilt am I to Marissa, Raven? I don't understand."

"She hasn't confided in me. I will only speak of what I see, Jefferson. Grief, guilt. The belief that, in some way she's responsible for the deaths of her husband and parents. Or that she could have prevented the tragedy. Most of all, she thinks it's wrong to feel, to care, especially to love again."

"When you lost your parents and your brother, did you think it was wrong to feel anything but guilt, Raven?"

She didn't reply for the length of a trembling breath. When she answered she was calm. "At first, I did. I hated the world. But I hated myself the most—for living, for feeling when my family never would again. But Simon had come for me and he brought me here to his mother, Rhea.

Together they wouldn't let me *not* survive. They wouldn't let me not be whole.''

''You think I can do that for Marissa?''

''Yes.'' She was adamant. ''More than anyone, for I think you've felt the same in your own life. I suspect you still do in some ways. Just go carefully. For your sake and Marissa's. In the end, you might be surprised what you reap in helping her.''

''You speak from experience,'' Jefferson suggested softly.

Raven didn't bother dissembling. ''David was troubled when Simon sent him to the valley. I was as recovered as I could be as a solitary woman. Together we found our way to the love and life we share today. It can be the same for you, Jefferson.''

''If I go carefully,'' he finished for her.

''Yes.'' A smile offered encouragement. ''Now I'll leave you to think and rest. Tomorrow promises to be a long day.''

She was at the steps of her own home when he called out. ''Raven, how will I know what to do?''

''That's the simplest part of all. Follow your heart, Jefferson Cade. Always and forever, follow your heart.''

Four

Jefferson brought his truck to a stop by a hangar, recalling another such structure that had housed the small jet flown cross-country by Rick Cahill. So much had happened, so much had changed, it didn't seem possible that the first flight had been only a little more than a week ago.

Slightly jet-lagged and weary from all that had transpired in those days, he looked at his watch. Mentally running through the agenda he'd been given, he was pleased. "Perfect timing. But what else would Simon McKinzie expect?"

Realizing that he was talking to himself again, instead of the horses and Satan as he was wont to do on the Broken Spur, he pushed open the door and swung to the ground. With the sun at his back, his stare searching the sky, he wasn't surprised when he heard the plane a second before he saw it. "Perfect timing again."

As Simon expected. The phrase rattled, unbidden, through

his brain. It was, he'd discovered, the code of Simon's men. Doing what the man who had drawn them to him required. Not just because it was what they'd been trained to do. But because it was what they wanted. For Simon, for themselves. Most of all for the safety of their country and its citizens.

For people like Marissa.

Jefferson paced, suddenly anxious. Though he knew this part of Simon's proposed itinerary would be executed as meticulously as his part had been. Proving his trust and easing his concern, in a matter of a few more minutes, a small corporate plane touched down and taxied almost to the hangar.

Jogging onto the runway, Jefferson waved at Yancey as if he were accustomed to seeing his friend in the pilot seat of first one aircraft and then another. When it came to The Black Watch, one quickly became accustomed to many things. And learned to expect anything and any hidden skill among its men.

When the passenger door opened, Jefferson was there to help Marissa. His hands spanning her waist, her body sliding against his like a caress, he set her down on the tarmac. Keeping her close within his embrace he recalled another time, another caress. Another land. As his fingers lingered over her ribs and with the fullness of her breast almost touching his chest, he smiled down at her. "Welcome to Arizona, Marissa."

"Thank you," she murmured and stepped out of the steadying protection of his arms with the aplomb of nobility.

Not sure if she was thanking him for sparing her the leap to the tarmac or the welcome, Jefferson turned to Yancey who circled the plane with a clipboard in hand. "Good flight?"

"When you're flying a sweet baby like this—" with an

easy move, Yancey tossed the clipboard inside the plane and secured the door Marissa had exited ''—it's always a good flight.''

''Another case of maintenance that won't happen? Or another plane that's not for sale?'' Jefferson drawled.

''This sale is legit.'' Yancey grinned as he leveled an approving gaze at the sleek craft. ''I'm delivering it as a favor to Patrick McCallum, a friend of Simon's.''

''The Scottish financier.'' It wasn't a question, proving Jefferson's surprise quotient. ''And strictly a favor?''

''Yes. Though there's a history there. One of Simon's own—a lady sharpshooter, to be exact—rescued Patrick's little daughter from a religious zealot. Patrick and Simon have also worn the Scottish kilts at more than a few of the same gatherings of the clans.'' Yancey grinned again and slid an arm about Marissa. Bringing her to him, he kissed the top of her head. ''If it worked for The Watch that I had this beautiful traveling companion, Patrick will only be delighted.''

''You know McCallum, too,'' Jefferson suggested.

''Our paths cross,'' Yancey admitted. ''Now and again.'' Stepping back from Marissa and offering a hand to Jefferson, his grin vanished. His brilliant green gaze held Jefferson's. ''Our Merrie's all grown up now, so you two take care of each other. Watch your step, Jeffie.''

''Count on it, Yance.'' There was warmth in the handclasp of old friends, and memories recalled in names of the past.

Patrick McCallum's new plane was in the air, a diminishing speck of silver flying into the sun that rode high above the horizon when Jefferson turned again to Marissa. ''We have hours of driving before we make the canyon. We should go.''

''Right,'' she agreed and would have taken the luggage

Yancey had left on the tarmac. Jefferson was there before her.

"After you." He waited until she turned, then together they crossed to his truck. Matching her long stride, he finished setting her bags in the bed of the truck in time to take her arm as she climbed into the passenger seat.

Marissa tensed, but didn't jerk away, and for the second time thanked him politely. When her door was closed, then his, she found being shut away from the world with only Jefferson was too intimate, too tempting. Though the truck was hardly the tree house, and Arizona's barren beauty bore little similarity to the lush lowcountry, memories came rushing back.

Memories that left her floundering, not sure what she felt, or should feel. Tension mounted and wore thin. A keening awareness scraped at raw nerves and crackled between them. An awareness as charged with emotion as it was unacknowledged.

Marissa's way of dealing with what she couldn't resolve was to huddle against the door, keeping her face toward the window. For hours she watched the stark and splendid vistas they passed by. In those hours she tried to block everything from her mind except how the play of changing light brought new and different grandeur to this vast land.

Jefferson turned twice and angled and skirted box canyons and washes countless times. Eventually the truck always headed due west again. Some roads were paved, some loose gravel, some hard-packed dirt. The first was nearly deserted. The last, totally deserted. Unless one counted a cow or two. Or the occasional small herd of horses. Twice she glimpsed a rooftop, then again a windmill. Another time, a small oil rig constantly churning. Each meant people. But none were visible.

"I should have known," Jefferson said, at last, in a voice rusty from disuse and dust.

Marissa didn't look away from the window, or from the sprawl of unbroken, empty land. When Jefferson thought she wouldn't break her interminable silence, she stirred and shifted, long legs stretching in the little space allowed. Though he concentrated on potholes and bumps and billowing dust, he could feel her gaze on him.

"What should you have known, Jefferson?" Her question was the first she'd asked. The first time she'd spoken since they left the private airfield.

Making the most of this break in her silence, he kept the conversation going. "I should have known Simon was too cautious to allow you to arrive by a straightforward, conventional route. The man thrives on intrigue. But, thank God he does."

"Yes." With that agreement, she resumed her mute study of the Arizona landscape.

"Yes?" He wanted to hear her voice more than an answer.

"I beg your pardon?"

"Yes, Simon's cautious? Yes, he thrives on intrigue? Or yes, thank God he does? Which is it, Marissa?"

She laughed. A husky, unconsciously seductive note. For a modicum of time, her tension eased. "All of the above."

"Yeah." He flashed a grin—for a beautiful woman, a father's daughter, a loyal wife. Even he didn't realize it was his first real grin in days. "Good call, sweetheart."

As she looked away, her hair fell from its center part to drape over her cheeks. Absently, with both hands, she raked it back, her fingers threading through it like a comb. Jefferson was fascinated by the way it fell so orderly to her shoulders once more. He was fascinated by the way the gesture lifted her breasts against the taut leather of her vest. Even with a road that demanded unwavering attention, it was hard not to steal a second glance at the curve of her narrow waist as it flowed into the slender line of her hips and thighs.

Except for concerned glances, he'd kept his gaze resolutely forward for the duration of this roughest part of the drive. But he'd been fiercely aware of everything about her from the moment she'd walked away from the plane.

Once they were sealed in the small cab of the truck, he sensed more than saw every move. Every slow, controlled breath that lifted her breasts against the vest.

He was aware of each rare and restless shift of her long legs. On the plain she'd worn leather. Today, new denim. Part of Raven's purchases made during a quick trip to Madison, a small college town near the valley.

The denim had been faded and softened by an artificial aging process. It was Simon's directive that Marissa's clothing not attract attention by marking her as a tenderfoot going Western with a new wardrobe.

"Didn't work."

The words were no more than a breath, his lips barely moving in a quirking smile. The worn, aged look that was supposed to make her blend like a native, drawing no inordinate attention to her, hadn't come close to the effect Simon wanted.

Instead the supple fabric clung to her lean body in ways that made a man enjoy watching her move in that gliding stride of taller, lithesome women. The dark red shirt, though slightly faded, too, was the perfect foil for her dark hair and tawny skin.

With her boots and hat and open vest, she could fit on any ranch. But she was too damn beautiful to go unnoticed.

Fighting the familiar surge of desire, gripping the steering wheel, Jefferson drove in silence. Leaving Marissa to her thoughts. Deliberately turning his to the trip home.

Home. This venture proved that after four years Arizona

had become home. And after the time away, it would be good to be back in the canyon. Good to see Satan again.

Perhaps that eagerness contributed to making today's journey interminable. The first part of his route from Simon's valley had been complicated. With secret stops and switches. Until the last, a commercial flight from Belle Terre. It was then he'd discovered his original tickets had been used, rather than canceled. Anyone curious enough or interested enough to make note of his arrival, or to check the point of origin of his flight, would assume he was returning from a visit with his family.

After he'd left the canyon with Rick, Billy had driven the truck to Phoenix. Leaving it in long-term airport parking gave credence to what the sheriff hoped would be the natural assumption that Jefferson had returned to the low-country for a few days.

Once he'd collected the truck from the airport, as instructed, he'd followed a circuitous route to the private landing strip to meet Marissa. Which left this final drive.

"Tired?" he asked as she sighed softly.

"Maybe a bit." The admission was made with a half smile.

"After weeks on the Argentine plain, the trip to the valley, then to the ranch, how could you not be? But I suspect it's more than a bit." Reaching out, his fingertips brushed briefly over her wrist. "But it won't be long now."

At his touch, memories she'd struggled to ward off wouldn't be denied. Bittersweet memories that made her body yearn for the touch of his weathered, brawny hands. Hands that were beautiful in their strength and tenderness. Gentle hands that could tease and seduce, leaving a trail of sweet, wanting flame with each caress. Knowing hands that incited needs and desire beyond imagining.

No one had ever touched her as Jefferson had. Never before. Never in the years since. Once she would have said that hadn't mattered. That the life Paulo had given her was enough. That freedom, education and his wise guidance compensated for the absence of vigor and passion. Then on the plain and in the valley, as she'd watched Jefferson through half-shuttered eyes, she'd known all she'd tried to believe was a lie.

Now, as she saw those powerful, virile hands guiding the truck skillfully over nearly impassable terrain, she remembered what she'd never truly forgotten. She understood that for as long as she lived she could never forget those roughened, beautiful hands, that could soothe and gentle the wildest of horses, had soothed and gentled an innocent young woman as he taught her the sweet secrets of passion.

"Hey, pretty lady. Penny for your thoughts."

Startled, ridiculously afraid he'd read her mind, she pressed her hands against the sudden rush of heat that burned her cheeks. Regaining her composure, when she faced him the guilt for her disloyal admission of the short-comings of her marriage to Paulo had begun its ugly taunts.

Ungrateful, selfish, cold. An adulteress in heart and mind, if not her body. A wicked woman who lusted for another man when her aged, benevolent husband had been dead only six weeks.

Puzzled, risking a look away from what had deteriorated into a body-battering track, Jefferson reached across the cab to trail the back of his hand over her cheek. "I didn't mean to upset you, sweetheart. I'm not sure what I said or did, but I'm sorry."

"Don't! Please don't!" Lurching beyond his reach, Marissa huddled against the door. Her hand gripping the handle as if she would flee if she could. But was any place far enough? Her breath was labored, the harsh sound of it filling the stunned silence of the truck. Gradually as it calmed, she released the handle and clasped her hands in her lap. Her posture was rigid, her eyes shadowed when she whispered in a voice brimming with regret, ''Don't be sorry, Jefferson. Not for anything. But, please, don't touch me again.''

The sun had slid behind the mountains, and though he could just barely see her face, he stared at her. Even in darkness he could comprehend her rigid posture, the wooden expression and interpret their message. ''Marissa, sweetheart…''

When she flinched at the endearment, his teeth clenched, his lips closed over questions he would have asked. Clutching the steering wheel harder, he stared through the dusty windshield, while he wondered how his life and hers would go from here.

He wanted to apologize for whatever sin he'd committed, but he knew she wouldn't listen. He wanted to brake the truck, to haul her into his lap and kiss away her pain and grief. Her fear.

But his endearment was offensive. His touch abhorrent.

Yet she hadn't minded that he touched her on the plain. Nor in the valley. What changed? What was different?

Separate silences settled over them as the truck continued its slow, bumpy path, its lights joining with moonlight to guide them. Marissa returned to her vigil of the land. If she'd really seen it, she would have discovered yet another facet of this endlessly changing terrain. But she didn't notice as she tried to forget what a fool she must seem to Jefferson.

After a searching look seeking answers, but finding her stiff and remote, Jefferson kept his eyes on the road ahead. But his thoughts were not as riveted on the road as his glaring stare.

Please, don't touch me.

Don't touch me.

Her cry was like an omen, a knell, sounding in his mind. At first, he'd thought he was mistaken when she'd drawn away so abruptly. But when he moved past the shock of her reaction, he knew it would take worse than a simpleton to misunderstand.

She couldn't bear to have him touch her. He had discovered this new Marissa was a quiet woman. Perhaps, withdrawn in her grief, even more quiet than usual. But until just now he hadn't sensed her loathing of the feel of his hands on her.

Loathing of him? Or of what he might want from her?

Then he understood. Even though it had been judged the safest of places for her, she hadn't wanted to come to the Broken Spur. Because that meant she would be alone with him. With her friends around, as Juan and Marta had been on the plain, or in the valley with Simon and his men never very far away, she was comfortable with him. At least comfortable enough to function.

"But never when we're alone." Jefferson didn't realize he'd muttered out loud through gritted teeth, until she finally faced him, a questioning frown drawing down her brows. "It was nothing," he assured her. "Just thinking."

"What were you thinking, Jefferson?" That she was insane? An ungrateful bitch? Was he regretting that he'd ever received her message? Didn't he have reason to, given her strange behavior? "It must be that I'm an ugly, insensitive person. Awful. Rude."

Her hands still clasped in her lap, her fingers twined over each other with a brutal force. "After you've done so much for me, stopping your life in midstride, abandoning your responsibilities...you must think I'm terribly ungrateful."

"You couldn't be ugly if you tried, Marissa. Or awful, or rude. And I don't want your gratitude." Pausing for breath, he recalled he'd said almost those exact words to her in the valley.

I don't want your gratitude, Marissa...in fact gratitude is the last thing I want.

"But that doesn't matter now." A jackrabbit bounded across the road. Braking and swerving to avoid it, he waited until the truck returned to an even keel before he continued. "The important thing is to get you settled in at the ranch. Then, within the next two weeks to a month, Juan and Marta will be moving to Jake's new property."

"Two weeks to a month. It seems as long as forever." Thankful for a change of subject, Marissa fought the urge to babble out her appreciation for this opportunity for Juan. Jefferson was indirectly responsible, but he wouldn't want her thanks for the Elias any more than he wanted it for herself. "I'll miss them, especially Alejandro."

"You love that little boy, don't you?"

She didn't answer. Then, her gaze locked on her tortured hands, she whispered, "As I would have loved my own son."

Jefferson heard another layer of grief in her voice. And he wondered if her life of wealth and influence had been so wonderful after all. Suddenly, he realized Señora Marissa Rei was a woman of secrets. Pain-filled secrets.

The need was there to touch her. To ease hidden hurts. Instead he settled for platitudes. "I know you didn't want to come here. But it's for the best. Once you've settled in and we get you on horseback, you'll find time flies in the canyon.

"And you *will* like it here, Marissa. I can promise you that, at least."

"Here?" Curious in spite of herself, she sat up straighter. Though she'd stared out the window hours on end, in the last miles her eyes had been blinded by thoughts turned inward. Now, gaze darting, she strained for a glimpse of the range she'd heard so much about. "We're on the Broken Spur?"

"Not quite, but at any second we will be."

"Then this is Benedict land." Even that was intriguing. She'd heard much of the Rafter B, and the Benedict empire.

"We've traveled across it for nearly four hours."

"That long? His land covers that great distance? Then it rivals some of the greatest *estancias* in Argentina."

"It's big," Jefferson agreed. "If Jake could've had his way a few years back, it would be bigger. And he would have what he's wanted for a long time. Steve Cody's Sunrise Canyon."

"Obviously he didn't get it." It was good to speak of something other than her own troubles, and the unthinking hurt she'd caused Jefferson. "What went wrong?"

"It shaped up to be quite a fracas. Then it wasn't."

"Because?" Marissa prodded when he said no more.

"Because Steve came away with all he ever wanted. The Broken Spur and Jake's daughter, Savannah."

"Savannah Cody. Savannah Benedict Cody, currently in England with her husband and their daughter Jakie." Marissa laughed softly. A sound as rare in her life now as it had been in Jefferson's. "A fairy tale come true."

"Not a fairy tale," Jefferson said. "A love story come true. Sure Steve ended up with the ranch and the woman he loved. But if he'd had to choose…"

"He would have chosen Savannah," she supplied, and was certain she was right.

"No contest."

"It turned out wrong for Jake Benedict, but right for everyone else."

"In the end, it was right for Jake, too. Thanks to Sandy Gannon and a baby called Jakie." But that was a story for another time Jefferson decided as he let the truck glide to a stop. He turned the key and stepped out. Crossing to her side, he opened the passenger door, careful not to touch her. "Come with me."

When she stood beside him he went with her, leading

her across rough and rugged ground to a precipice. Without taking her arm, as it had been drummed into him all his life he should. Old habits of Southern gentlemen died hard, but he was learning.

He hadn't planned to arrive just as the moon struck the stream, turning it to a ribbon of silver, but he had. A globe of cold fire, its light filled the canyon where the grass was belly deep and only a few horses grazed, waiting for the rest of the herd to come from a pasture deeper in the canyon.

A barn huddled a little away from the stream. Beyond a grove of aspen, the house that had been no more than a cabin, lay in darkness. The hand Sandy sent to fill in had finished the day's chores and returned to the Rafter B for the night.

His gesture swept over the entire vista. "Welcome to Sunrise Canyon and the Broken Spur, Marissa. The home of Steve and Savannah Cody. And—for a while—yours as well."

She was quiet as she looked from one side of the canyon to the ridge of the precipice where they stood. Far longer than it was wide, and with water plentiful and good grass, it was a natural corral. Perfect for horses and for a woman who loved them. Perfect, Jefferson was certain, for this woman who needed a place to heal. A refuge, not just from the man who posed the threat, but from herself and what she believed. What she feared.

Jefferson hoped the healing had begun when she looked up at him and smiled. A small smile, a gentle lift of the corners of her mouth. No more. But for the first time, there was pleasure not tinged with hurt and grief.

Turning back to look again at the canyon, she was still smiling. "It's beautiful, Jefferson."

"Yes." As he agreed he knew it was right she'd come.

* * *

Viewed from the canyon floor, Steve Cody's land was no less spectacular. As she stood by the truck, Marissa turned in a slow circle. "It's no wonder Jake Benedict wanted this. No matter how much land he might have, any cattleman would want this. But I expected the operation would be larger."

"It could have been. At first, even though the land was a gift, money was a factor. Steve did all the work himself, unless a neighboring cowhand happened by to lend a hand now and then."

"One of them called Jeffie?"

"I pitched in a few times. So did Sandy Gannon. For that matter, even when they were at war with neither admitting what they felt for each other, so did Savannah."

"You make it sound more and more like quite a love story."

"Yeah." Moving away from her because he couldn't stand so close and not touch her, Jefferson searched the gloom beneath a tree. "There's someone I'd like you to meet."

"Here?" The house was dark. The stables, quiet. No unexpected arrival disturbed the grazing horses. "Now?"

"Here and now. His name is Satan. I think you're going to like him. I know he'll love you."

"He." Her head tilted. But as in the valley by the lake, his face was in shadow. Softly she repeated the unusual name. "Satan."

Finding pleasure in the verbal fencing that recalled their time together during her years at the university in Belle Terre, Jefferson grinned. "Satan."

"How many legs would Satan happen to have?" Before he could answer, she stopped him with her hand up, palm facing him. "No, let me guess—four."

"Good guess."

"Satan's a male name. Would he be in the barn?"

Propping a forearm against the truck, Jefferson loomed over her. His fingers nearly brushed a curling tendril at her temple, before he thought to draw them back. It would be so easy to succumb to the desire to slide his fingers through the dark wealth of her hair. But she'd laid down the rules of her stay, and he would abide by them, even if it killed him. "Satan can be in the barn, at times. But not usually."

"Not a Cody stud," she ventured. "Not a horse at all."

A slight tilt of his head and a drawl acknowledged she was on target. "Not a horse."

"I don't think you're a cat man." With narrowed eyes, she considered that. "Not unless it was a bobcat." A shake of her head set her hair stirring against her shoulders and the scent of it surrounded him. "But not with horses. And that leaves...a dog."

Jefferson answered with a shrill whistle. After two sharp trills, Satan's deep bark rumbled, then he whimpered as the pads of his massive feet pounded the red earth.

Because Satan was the color of night, Marissa saw little more than a black shape hurling itself at Jefferson. As man and beast went down, she heard laughter.

When the wrestled greeting ended and Jefferson had cuffed the great dog affectionately on its massive head, he got to his feet. A little out of breath he made the introductions. "Marissa, meet Satan."

Fearlessly delighted, she was down on Satan's level immediately. Crouched in the dust she was eye-to-eye with the magnificent creature. "Hello, Satan." Petting fingers stroked the long Doberman jaw. "I'm glad to make your acquaintance."

Jefferson tensed while Satan shivered and danced in place. But as Marissa continued to croon to the Doberman, he realized that the massive dog looked like a puppy falling under her spell. By the time she rose to stand next to him,

Jefferson knew the Dobie had fallen completely in love with her.

A common male occurrence, he thought wryly as he watched them form a mutual admiration society. "If I can tear you away from each other, it's time to show Marissa her new home."

Together they walked to the cabin. Marissa and Jefferson, with Satan between them. When Jefferson opened the door, Satan waited, determined to enter, but only after his new love.

Jefferson knew Satan had just acquired himself another human. From this day, he would be Marissa's constant companion, her protector. Added insurance that wouldn't hurt at all.

When he'd shown her to her upstairs bedroom, Satan was by her side. With her permission, he was still there when Jefferson returned to the first floor and his own bedroom.

Where long into the night, he lay sleepless, thinking about Marissa, the woman who was only a forbidden touch away.

Five

"**O**uch and be damned!"

Angry at himself for his carelessness, Jefferson dashed blood from his hand and returned his attention to the strand of barbed wire he was repairing. Where his attention should've been all along. "Except," he muttered taking a bandanna from his hip pocket to bind around his palm when the furrow across it bled profusely.

"Yeah, *except*." Except he couldn't keep his eyes off Marissa. The bandanna slipped, and he bit back another oath.

She'd been in the canyon two weeks. And for two weeks they'd kept a careful truce. By tacit agreement, they didn't discuss her life or his life, the past, the present, the future. Nothing more personal than the responsibilities that were part of ranch life.

"Tiptoeing, like strangers." With that low growl, his gaze lifted again to Marissa. Admiring her, and her spirit.

She'd certainly assumed a healthy share of the workload that was involved in the daily routine of ranching, and raising and training horses. Beginning with her first day in the canyon. When he expected she would sleep late, or at least rest, she was the first up and moving about the kitchen as if she'd never been tired, much less exhausted. As if she were quite at home on the Broken Spur.

Jefferson remembered that odd little lurch he'd felt when he'd stepped into the kitchen that first morning. Whatever he might have expected to discover it wouldn't have been a beautiful woman just taking a pan of biscuits from the oven. Five minutes later, he'd been seated at the table, a cup of coffee in his hand and a plate filled with bacon and scrambled eggs set before him.

"Earning my keep. It's the only way this is going to go," she'd told him when he protested. The pleasant words and a determined look ended that discussion effectively and forever.

Each day thereafter, breakfast was on the table promptly at five-thirty. Before he left the house, leftovers of bacon or sausage or whatever, were wrapped and ready for a lunch on the move. As he'd told her was his custom. Supper was never fancy, but she had a way of making plain fare not so plain. It was plentiful, and always ready at the end of each long grueling day.

Through it all, they observed a careful truce, and he never touched her. "Tiptoeing." How else could they go? How long?

When the blood had been stanched, or at least slowed to an ooze, he wrapped the bandanna more loosely around his palm, looped it clumsily with his right hand, then held the cloth with his teeth to secure a knot. Satisfied the makeshift bandage would suffice, he glanced one more time at the corral where Marissa put the new filly through the first paces of her training.

Marissa in action was a sight to behold. But Jefferson needed to concentrate on his own set of chores, for beholding the sight of her had led to his confrontation with the barbed wire. Turning away, thankful this was the last broken strand, he made quick work of it. Between the resounding strikes of his hammer, he could hear her low croon. He couldn't distinguish the words, but he knew by rote the string of constant instruction and praise she chanted as she taught the filly the first of a number of skills.

When the repair was finished, Jefferson gathered his tools and stowed them in a small toolbox. Stretching the ache from strained shoulders, he glanced at the sun, judging the time. Almost noon, time to knock off for lunch. The day that had begun early and would run late, was hot and would be hotter in an hour or so. The filly shouldn't do much more. But he wouldn't interfere. Marissa was as aware of the dangers of overheating as he.

And as he, she was inclined to take better care of the horses than of herself. Conscious of his own formidable thirst, foregoing the thermos he'd tucked into the toolbox, he crossed to the stream where the water ran clear and deep before separating into two branches. One meandered through fenced pastures. One veered past a grove of trees, then by the house.

He'd discovered that at this exact spot, the water was sweetest. Kneeling on one knee in the shade of an overhanging cottonwood tree, with his good hand he scooped up a palmful and drank. Thirst quenched, flinging aside his hat and the bandanna, he cleaned his wound, then splashed his face and head. As the cooling liquid sluiced down his arm and his body, he found his gaze returning to the corral, seeking out Marissa.

The corral was empty. As he'd known she would before long, she'd completed this training session, then had taken the filly to the barn. His hand rebound, returning to the fence, he gathered up the toolbox, mounted his ground-tied mare and cantered to the barn. To her.

"Good girl." Marissa petted the filly as she combed and curried her. "You're a pretty thing. Smart, too. Not to mention a bloodline that ranks with the royalty of horses. Gitano or Black Jack, or both, should get excellent colts on you."

The scuff of a boot heel, the whisper of cloth against cloth, caught her attention. Looking toward the barn door, she saw him standing there. Her hands went still. Her crooning faltered. Silence amplified by the tramp of horses and the creak of wood was broken only by the thunder of her heart. "Jefferson."

With sunlight at his back, he was only a dark figure. His hat was tilted over his forehead, shading an already shaded face, yet she felt the weight of his stare. Broad of shoulders, narrow-hipped, he was lean and strong in jeans that hugged his thighs before being drawn over boots with worn heels bearing a star.

There had never been anyone like him. There couldn't be. Inexplicably nervous, clasping the currycomb, she rested her hand on the filly's neck. "How long have you been there?"

"Not long." Long enough to see the gentleness in her as she cooled the horse and groomed it. She'd made a pet of every creature on the ranch. Including Gitano, Steve's Spanish stallion. And especially Black Jack, Savannah's mount—half wild, half mountain goat, all horse, the stallion had been moody and had moped around missing Savannah. Until Marissa had arrived.

"Where's your shadow?" He referred to Satan, the most besotted of the lot. Next to Jefferson Cade, he amended.

"He must have grown bored while I worked with the pretty girl." Laying comb and brush aside, she led the filly into a stall and closed the door. Facing Jefferson again, she explained. "He scurried off a little while ago. Chasing a roadrunner."

Jefferson chuckled. "He never learns. But if he should catch one, he wouldn't know what to do with it. I doubt bird or feathers are his favorite food."

"Has he ever caught one?"

"Never. Doesn't matter. The chase is the fun of it for Satan." The animals, always their safest subject. Something to keep his mind diverted from what he wanted. *What he wanted*... In an ungoverned impulse he asked, "Have you had lunch, Marissa?"

The abrupt shift surprised her. Frowning, she searched for an idea of the time and drew a blank. "Is it time already?"

"Past time." He moved closer. "It's also past time I checked the herd deeper in the canyon. Since you haven't seen more than the main part of the ranch, I thought you might grab a biscuit and ride along. There's a nice spot for a picnic."

Marissa had wanted to ride through more of the canyon. She'd wanted to ride with Jefferson. She'd wanted it for a long time. As he waited for her answer he moved closer, gradually becoming more than a dark familiar shape. He was color and light, wickedly rugged, wickedly handsome. She could think of nothing but Jefferson. There was only here and now, with the past and its grief and guilt forgotten in the thunder of her heart. But if he had work to do, she shouldn't hamper him. "Maybe you'd do best alone."

"It isn't wise to leave you." With his uninjured hand, he pushed his hat back. His blue gaze was more than brilliant. More than riveting. "Even with Satan on sentry duty."

"I see." Disappointment she tried to deny constricted her throat. He'd asked out of obligation. Not because he wanted to ride with her. But why should she expect it would be different? She'd treated him more like an enemy than a friend. The fault was hers, yet he'd borne the brunt of it.

She'd allowed it with her silence. But how could a woman thought to be a wife and widowed such a short time explain the need, the awakening of long-dormant desire so soon after her husband's death? Wouldn't the man she lusted for feel disgust for one so unfaithful, even if only to an arrangement and a memory?

"Marissa?"

He moved closer, questioning her silence. Bringing with him the fragrance of the out-of-doors to mingle with the scent of hay, horses and leather. The fragrance and scent that never failed to bring him to mind, no matter where she was. A pleasing scent that made her wish for... No! She spun away, turning her back on him. She mustn't let her mind wander where it wanted to go.

Laying the bridle aside, she reached out to take the saddle from the rail where she'd left it. Jefferson was there before her and she could only watch as he took it to the tack room.

Seconds later, he was back, looming over her, jogging her memory with his presence as much as his words. "The ride, Marissa," he prompted. "Would you like to go into the canyon?"

"I...no." Her eyes were downcast. Then, for no reason she could explain and casting caution aside, reversing her choice, she lifted her gaze to meet his. "Yes." Her voice was steady, her tone emphatic as she reached deep for the courage that had sustained her through other times of her life. Some as difficult. Others far more. "Yes, I'd like to ride with you, Jefferson."

Jefferson made no comment on her change of heart as he reached for a pair of bridles hanging outside the tack room door. "I'll get Black Jack and The Lady from the pasture. The Lady is Savannah's favorite next to Black Jack, and as surefooted as the stallion. I'll have them saddled and waiting when you're ready."

He was transferring the bridles to his left hand when Marissa gasped. Forgetting rules she'd laid down for herself and for him, she caught his wrist. "Jefferson!" Her eyes were riveted on the bandanna soaked in red. As she brought his hand with its bloody bandage closer, there was horror on her face. "What happened?"

"Got bit by a stubborn strand of barbed wire." Lifting a shoulder in dismissal, he smiled ruefully. "Goes with the territory. There are days that if I met the man responsible for inventing the damnable stuff, I'd shoot him."

"Stop it." She was frowning and cradling his hand in hers. "Don't make light of this. Surely you know an injury like this is dangerous and no joking matter." Then the desperate, worried questions poured out. "Have you had a tetanus vaccine recently? How deep did the barb go? Did you clean it? You could get an infection, or worse. Why didn't you tell me? I could have helped. I would have. Surely you know that."

When her worried tirade died more from lack of breath than questions, a pleased, deliberate grin curled Jefferson's lips. "Are you all done fussing over me? If you are, I'll explain."

"I've just begun fussing, as you say. But I'll listen to your excuses." She swept a doubtful look over him. "If you have any."

Her fingers still circled his wrist, as if he might run from her. When the last thing Jefferson wanted was to run. Standing compliantly in her grasp he addressed her questions in perfect order. "I know an injury such as this is nothing to blow off. I had a tetanus vaccine last year, providing immunity for several years. The barb didn't go deep, so much as it grabbed and ripped.''

He caught a breath. ''I cleaned it in the stream because, of course, I know it could become infected. I didn't tell you because I didn't want to interrupt your session with the filly.

''And, yes,'' he finished softly. ''I knew you could help, Marissa. I knew you would.''

''But you didn't ask.''

''I'm a big boy, now, sweetheart. I've lived here alone for over a year, and I was taking care of myself pretty well even before then.'' The endearment hadn't been intentional. But once spoken, it felt natural. Better yet, this time she didn't flinch. His grin grew. Hope for better days rippled through him. ''Maybe I've been too alone for too long,'' he added thoughtfully. ''If you'd like to fuss a little more, be my guest.''

''I intend to.'' Practically dragging him to the house, the dangers of living a lonely, isolated life were too clear to her. Too frightening. A horse could throw him, or roll on him. A snake could bite him. A rock could tumble from the rim of the canyon.

The mental tabulation of dangers would have grown, but with the falling rock, they arrived at the steps of the house. When he had been marched up the last stair and directed to sit at the kitchen table and wait, he sat at the table and waited.

There were first-aid supplies in the pantry off the kitchen. In no time, she was back. Dumping what she'd collected on the table, she left him again to fill a basin with warm water. With a towel and soap, she returned to the table. Sitting catercorner from him, her knees brushing his, she untied and unwrapped his hand, groaning. ''The wire did a number on you.''

"It snapped." The terse explanation was enough. Both were familiar with the rapid recoil of wire that lost tension.

"In that case, it's fortunate that this is the worst of it." She went to work on his wound. First, soaking his hand. Then bathing it with soapy disinfectant. "I don't want to hurt you."

"You won't, sweetheart." His voice was deep, a whisper.

Gradually her hands ceased moving. Then were still, cradling his. When she lifted her head, she found him waiting for her. Brown eyes held blue. Seeking. Perhaps finding.

After a time, he smiled. "You never have, you know."

Marissa couldn't respond. She didn't know what she felt or what she should say. Yet she didn't look away until Jefferson turned his hand clasping hers. Soberly, but with humor glinting in his eyes, he murmured, "Think I'm gonna to live, doc?"

Snapping back to real time, she said, "You might. After I paint this with antiseptic, and if you keep the bandage clean."

"That stuff stings, but I'll try to be brave."

"I'm sure you will be." Her tone was serious while his teased. "You always have been."

She was winding the last length of gauze around his palm when he commented on her skill. "You know what you're doing, don't you, Marissa? If I'd needed stitches you could have done them."

It wasn't a question but she answered. "I've studied medicine. Mostly obstetrics, to help on the *estancias*. Though practicing was never an option, I completed my studies…" Her voice broke, yet she continued her explanation. "I had completed the course. The trip was to be a celebration. When Alejandro fell ill, I planned to join Paulo and my parents later."

Jefferson wanted to take her in his arms. He wanted to

hold her and make her believe that with her or without her aboard, the plane would have crashed. And none of it was her fault. But it wasn't something he could make her believe with one embrace, one denial. It needed time, and that time was not now. Instead he addressed her studies. "You studied to learn, but never to practice. Your husband's blessing didn't quite embrace a career."

"He was very much of the old school where women were concerned. But he was a good man, Jefferson. Generous to a fault. Kinder and more forgiving than I deserved." The bandage was finished, the tape in place. There was no more reason to touch him. "Whatever sham our marriage might have been, Paulo was kind and forgiving, and always supportive."

"Kind, forgiving," Jefferson mused quietly. "You've used those words twice, almost in one breath."

Marissa didn't explain. "He was that sort of man."

"But you didn't love him." It had taken time to figure it out. But it was the only answer for her behavior. He met her startled look, seeing an answering regret in her expression. It would hurt to speak the words. Yet, like a festering wound, it would hurt more if she didn't. "Did you love him, Marissa?"

Color drained from her face, the pallor turning her eyes lightless black and bottomless. "Of course I loved him." Her voice shook and there was grief in the sound. "To know Paulo was to love him. Everybody who knew him loved him."

"Everybody loved him. You loved him." Her father's friend had been good to her. In her words, kind. For that, he was grateful. Marissa was a caring woman. She would respond to Rei's kindness. But Jefferson went with his gut feeling.

"You loved Paulo Rei." A clock on the mantel ticked

off seconds before he finished. "But you weren't in love with him."

Marissa stood hastily. Her chair tilted but righted at last. With competent hands only a little unsteady, she gathered up the first-aid supplies and repacked them into the kit. When that was done to her satisfaction, she took the basin to the sink to rinse it. Next she returned the kit to the pantry.

As he followed every move she made with interest, it wasn't difficult to imagine her serving as an over-trained medic working among the people of far-flung *estancias*. Something he suspected, she would prefer over an official medical practice. She was good. Damned good. But she hadn't answered his question.

She'd just stepped from the pantry, when he spoke again, taking up his conversation where it had broken off. "Were you, Marissa?" She stopped in midstride, her face still pale, her eyes still dark with grief. "Were you ever in love with Paulo Rei?"

She drew that long breath she needed to gather courage. "No, Jefferson." Her voice was calm. Too calm. "I was never in love with Paulo. Ours wasn't that sort of relationship."

That, he knew instinctively, was a great part of her guilt. A sham; she'd called her marriage a sham, and described it as not *that* sort of relationship. There were questions he would ask. But not now when she was so distraught. Rising from the table, he flexed the fingers of his injured hand. "Thank you for this, Marissa. It feels better already. If you're still interested in that ride?" Pausing, he waited only for her slow, silent nod. "I'll saddle Black Jack and The Lady. We'll be ready when you are."

Marissa tarried, wondering what she'd done. Long after his footsteps faded from the porch and the steps, she returned to the pantry to scavenge its shelves for an impromptu picnic.

The trail was an uneven track ever climbing, snaking past boulders and clumps of scrub and sparse cacti. As Marissa followed Jefferson, she could see that it was a route constantly changing. The soil was a mix of crumbling detritus, sandlike soil, or hard packed red earth. Some parts of it were wide, easily navigated, others were narrow, with jutting rock formations threatening a knee or ankle. But the threats never came to pass, thanks to Jefferson's guidance and softly called warnings.

When the idea of this ride had first been presented, she hadn't voiced her questioning of his choice of Black Jack over Gitano. Now, the black horse proved Jefferson's wisdom.

Black Jack was the most surefooted horse she'd ever seen. With The Lady coming in a close second. Only Satan, ranging ahead of them was surer. The filly she had worked with all morning hadn't been exposed to the trails, but there was something about the way she moved. "She could do this."

Jefferson turned in the saddle. "Something wrong?"

Realizing that she'd spoken her thoughts, Marissa shook her head. "Just thinking out loud."

"Care to share?" Beneath the brim of his hat, his eyes were stunning, as blue as the unclouded sky.

Eyes that could make any woman shiver in anticipation of the thoughts that clear steady gaze inspired. But certainly none she could, or should speak of. "I was thinking of the filly." Not quite a lie, not the full truth. "There's something about the way she walks. I can't explain it, but my intuition says she will make an excellent mountain horse. At least as good as The Lady."

Jefferson respected Marissa's horse sense. As much as

anyone he knew short of Sandy Gannon, Steve Cody, or Jesse Lee. And Savannah was no slouch. He wouldn't presume to second-guess any of them. Especially Marissa. Threading his reins through his gloved fingers, he leaned on the pommel of his saddle, his gaze keeping hers. "When you think she's ready, we'll bring her into the canyon. It's a good test for mountain horses."

"When she's ready," Marissa agreed. "If I'm still here."

Jefferson tensed, Black Jack responded to the change in his bearing by dancing restlessly in place. With a touch of a hand and a softly spoken word, the stallion was calmed.

Marissa watched as he stroked the horse. As his long, gloved fingers moved over Black Jack's sleek, black hide, there was gentleness in the stroke that controlled more than force or power. That was his way. As natural to Jefferson as breathing. A power greater than brute force.

His brothers had been brawlers. Known as boys, then men, who never instigated a controversy but were always standing in the end. Jefferson's one foray into battle ended with Adams Cade going to prison. Marissa knew Jefferson had been barely in his teens when he'd taken it upon himself to avenge an insult. He was too young, too inexperienced, to handle the issue. Adams had gone after him. What happened then lay shrouded in mystery for years.

Though she'd heard gossip, she'd been too young also. And too new to Belle Terre to understand all that happened. Except Adams was locked away and Jefferson banished himself in the swamp. In time the truth was revealed, Adams was exonerated.

All was forgiven. Except by Jefferson, who had never forgiven himself. In the time they'd spent together, pals, best of friends, roaming the land, this was the one subject of which he never spoke. Though it changed his life irrevocably, causing him to exile himself from his brothers, he had never explained.

She knew the truth. That the oldest and the youngest of the Cade brothers had truly saved each other that night. She'd never heard it from Jefferson's guilt-ridden perspective. She'd never questioned him, she never would. But she realized now, on a dusty trail far removed from the Carolina lowcountry, that she very much wanted to hear the story in his own words.

Then she would understand this good man. Because they were so alike. Because they both bore the brunt of tragedy, maybe in understanding Jefferson, she could understand herself.

She watched his fingers trailing over Black Jack, soothing the spirited creature. He'd done the same for her that final day in the swamp. He'd given her the accord she'd sought, courage to do what she must. He would again, if she'd let him.

His hands were magic, their caress a gift of courage and peace. His gift, honed by tragedy. Given to all but himself.

Dust that billowed in a red cloud beneath the stallion's hooves began to settle. The upheaval was finished, when Jefferson spoke again. "There's one bad patch left on the trail. But from there, barring a new slide, or a collapsing rock formation, it should be downhill and easy the rest of the way."

Black Jack stamped a foot, eager to move on. The Lady responded with a toss of her head. Jefferson smiled, reading the message they sent. "Ready?"

"I'm ready." She wasn't quite sure for what, or when. But something inside her was changing, shifting. Something that couldn't be hurried. "Or I will be." Her words were quiet, lost in the clatter of hooves on rocky ground. "One day. Soon."

* * *

Confident of her ability, and The Lady's, Jefferson set Black Jack into a gallop. With dust flying again, they rode in silence, enjoying the moment. At the crest of this last rise, the trail began a sharp descent. Twisting, nearly looping back on itself, it descended again into the protective shade of canyon walls. Brush thrived and thickened, nearly blocking the narrow, little used trail in places. And as they moved deeper into this secluded part of Sunrise Canyon, the sound of tumbling water was a welcome intrusion into the quiet of the trail.

One strand of wire stretching across the trail turned the arroyo into a natural corral. Jefferson's quick dismount, a shift of fencing, then when she'd ridden past it leading Black Jack, the reconnection of wire, and they were in. Secure in a tiny world of every color of the spectrum. A feast for the senses.

"Take a look around," Jefferson suggested. "I'll check the horses, then meet you by the stream." He looked down at her, struggling against the compelling urge to touch her. Against the need to kiss her. With his look tracing the shape of her mouth, he asked, "Have you worked up an appetite?"

"Yes." Her answer was automatic. But she discovered she was looking forward to eating, as she hadn't been since the day her family died. "I'll set out what I put in the saddlebag. I'm sorry it isn't more. Where would you like it?"

"Anything will be fine. Anywhere you choose will be fine." Backing away while he could, he hurried to the horses. Leaving her questioning the sudden edge in his voice.

In this tranquil place, after a challenging ride that should have worked off lingering tension, he seemed ill at ease. He was striding past boulders that would hide him from her sight, before she turned to the stream to seek out a place for a picnic.

The site she chose was shaded by the spreading limbs of a cottonwood. There were only biscuits and bacon from the morning, along with a thermos of the strong, black coffee he liked. With another of the cool, sweet water from the stream for her. Makeshift fare, spread on a tattered blanket. But neither he nor she were prone to great feasts in the middle of a hot, dusty workday when it was thirst, not appetite that needed quenching.

When she finished, she sat down to wait for Jefferson's return, and a sense of peace surrounded her as she listened to the whisper of a breeze in the cottonwood. A perfect accompaniment for the babble of the stream. Jefferson's footsteps sounded behind her, but she didn't turn. With her gaze ranging this unexpected place, she murmured, "This is beautiful."

"Yes," he said simply. But he only had eyes for Marissa as he came down beside her.

"The horses?"

"No problems. The grass here is good, but we should consider moving them in a week or so."

We. He spoke to her as his partner. "Will we need help?"

"They've done this enough that they know the trail. One hand could do it. Two makes it easier. But that's enough."

"Hungry?"

"Am I?" He laughed, a rare husky sound touched by strain. Dear heaven, yes he was hungry. Hungrier than he'd ever been or thought he could be. He was too hungry here in this secluded paradise. But not for food. "Yeah," he muttered. "As a bear."

"A bear?" Her speculative gaze ranging over him not helping his situation, "A wolf maybe, or a tiger, or even the bobcat like before. But I could never see you as a bear.'' The beginning of a smile faltered as she saw the bloody bandage on his left hand. ''Jefferson, you're bleeding again!''

''It's nothing.'' Her fingertips barely brushed his wrist when he jerked away. ''Don't! Don't touch me, Marissa. Not here. Dear God, not now.''

Her hand hovered between them, then dropped to her knee. The flush of color the ride had brought to her cheeks faded. The pleasure she'd found in this wild and wonderful place that matched the aura of the lowcountry vanished. ''I suppose I deserved that.'' Her voice was raw, brittle. ''I'm sorry.''

Wishing he'd bitten his tongue rather than spoken to her as he had, he searched for a way to make her understand.

''After the way I behaved on the drive to the canyon, I can't blame you for not wanting me to touch you, Jefferson.''

''Not wanting you to touch me? Is that what you think this is about?'' He wanted to lift her face to his. But he dared not. Instead, he said, ''Look at me, Marissa. Look in my eyes, see for yourself and believe that I want your touch. See and believe that I want far more. More than you're ready to give.''

''You're not angry about what I said?'' Her dark eyes searched his, and saw no condemnation.

''I was never angry. Puzzled, yes. Then, after a while, I understood. You've a long way to go in resolving your grief. But, just so you understand, I want you, Marissa. I want your touch, your kiss. I want the love, and yes, the lust. I want it all, Marissa. Everything. But not before its time.

''I don't want to rush you, sweetheart. But if that day in the swamp didn't mean what I thought it meant, if you didn't love me then, tell me now.''

There it was. Dragging in a long breath, Marissa closed

her eyes. Shutting out everything, but the one thing she couldn't deny. Right or wrong. Reprehensible or not—the truth. "I can't."

"Can't?" he prompted gently, patiently, leaving countless questions unasked.

She turned to him, staring up at him. "I can't tell you that you were wrong. I can't tell you I didn't love you."

Forgetting his hand and breaking rules that no longer applied, Jefferson reached for her then. Folding her into his embrace as she came willingly to him, he held her. "That's a beginning and enough for now." His lips brushed her hair as he whispered a promise. "We'll work it out. Maybe sooner, maybe later, but we will work this out.

"All of it," he added grimly as thoughts of Menendez turned his tenderness to anger.

Six

"**A**h-h." With that groan of relief, dusty, soaked with sweat, body stiff and refusing to obey, Marissa fell out of the saddle. More a gangly landing than her usual easy dismount. Her legs nearly buckling, with another groan she straightened, discovering the exhilarated pleasure in every taut, aching muscle.

Her day had begun as days always began on the ranch. Awake by five. Breakfast by five-thirty. In the barn tending and feeding horses by six. Next a session with the pretty mare she'd begun calling Bonita. A session that had run long today. Not because the surefooted horse was having difficulty, but because Marissa sensed her agile and cooperative mount was enjoying the routine. Bonita was proving to be a unique horse. A hard worker, a quick learner. Patient. A mount that shared a rapport with its rider.

When the session ended the sun was high, the early summer temperature soaring. It was time. Time to ride again with Jefferson to the *ciénaga*. This, he had explained at the end of their first trip farther into the land of the Broken Spur, was the name Savannah Henrietta Benedict Cody had given that distant part of the canyon when she was still a young girl. A very young girl called Hank, not Savannah, who found it a respite from the often impossible burden of being Jake Benedict's only child.

The most isolated part of the canyon would never by any stretch of the imagination truly be a marshland. But, for Marissa, in mood and spirit, the Spanish name fit.

She'd come away from it the first time with the beginning of a better perspective. Nothing concrete. A change sensed rather than understood. A cornerstone for building toward a new outlook, a new life. A paradoxical feeling of history repeating itself as Jefferson shared the healing serenity of a desert paradise as kindly and gently as he had in the lowcountry.

The first ride in had been a time of exploring the canyon. A part of a normal workday coupled with the pleasure of discovery. Today had been strictly labor. As a team they'd worked together, Jefferson and she, driving the herd pastured there back home.

Though the roundup was strenuous, keeping the horses on the trail as a whole hadn't been difficult. But there was always the wanderer that would stray past an outcropping of boulders or through a copse of brush. Or straight up an impossible incline. But The Lady was always willing to follow, and Satan helped.

Through the day, Marissa whistled and called until her throat was parched. She'd stretched and strained, riding her stirrups until her legs trembled. Her hat and her hair, drawn back in a ponytail, were covered in a film of red dust. Her face was marked and streaked with that same dust mingled with sweat. When she clenched her teeth grit ground between them.

As she stripped the saddle from The Lady and led her for a short drink, she was as hot and exhausted as her mount. As she took off her hat, dragged the tie from her hair and wiped the back of her gloved hand over her forehead, she'd never felt so good.

Leaving the horse to rest, she walked to the corral fence. Leaning against the top rail, she watched the new herd mill among the old. A result, in part, of her efforts. Body-battering, unglamorous work. She laughed, a contented sound.

"A pretty sight, isn't it?" His own mount unsaddled and watered, Jefferson had come to stand beside her. He was as dusty, perhaps as exhausted, but in him there was a glow of fulfillment. Together they watched the herd.

Standing beside him at the end of a day of accomplishment made the concerted effort even more satisfying. Turning her gaze from the herd, absorbing the look of him—the dark blond hair, streaked with silver and barely visible beneath his hat. Broad shoulders made broader by work and life and time. A lean torso, flat belly, powerful thighs and long, muscular legs, all blending into an arresting and beautiful man.

It was all a part of Thomas Jefferson Cade. A man who had come for her when she needed him. Who shared this moment with her. "I can't think of anything or any place prettier."

"Rough day?" he asked, though there was no question in his tone. "Have I demanded too much of you, sweetheart?"

Sweetheart. He called her that routinely now. But she'd never gotten accustomed to the endearment. Even in her grief and guilt, a warm sensation never failed to settle in the pit of her stomach. Though she'd learned to keep her hands and gaze steady, with that single word, he made her serene demeanor a lie.

"Rough, but good." Brushing a sweat soaked strand of hair from her cheek, she saw his concern. "You haven't demanded too much of me, Jefferson. You never have. It feels good to be useful. I rode often when Paulo and my parents were alive."

"But, as the wife of a wealthy man only for pleasure," he finished for her. "Rarely grueling work like this."

"No." The Lady had come to snuffle at her shoulder. Marissa stroked the mare and sighed a contented sigh. "Rarely like this. Of course there were occasions when I got away to the *estancia.* Beyond prying, watchful eyes, I rode less sedately."

"Especially with Juan."

"With Juan I could be myself. Rissa, as he has called me since my fifth birthday." Her hands clenched one over the other in painful remembrance. "My mother's illness had just been diagnosed. My father was wrapped up in her and in his business problems. I was always in the way. An energetic child who was too much for an ailing mother and a busy father.

"My father decided to channel the energy into a new passion. Horses was the obvious solution. Juan was young, but the best rider on the *estancia.* I was given into his care on that day."

"Not a bad choice." Jefferson had never met the Alexandres and he could never forgive them for bartering their daughter for wealth and security for themselves. But in their self-absorption, they'd given her a lifelong gift in Juan.

"Even with Juan's help, I wasn't the perfect daughter my parents needed," Marissa continued her reminiscence. "In my waywardness, I was a burden. But never for Juan. He expected no more or no less of me than that I be who I really was. He knew me as well as I knew myself, and understood me better than anyone else."

Her head turned, her eyes lifted to Jefferson's, seeing again the man who was everything she ever wanted. Everything she'd been denied. There was an ache in her voice for things lost as she whispered softly, "Better than anyone, except you."

Jefferson didn't move, he didn't respond. Though it took every iota of his willpower, he didn't reach for her. He didn't draw her into his arms, shushing her, soothing her anguish as he would have with any other hurting creature. But this was Marissa. As painful as her revelation must be, as painful as it was for him to let her endure this, it needed to be said.

When it was done, from the exorcism of guilt and pain would come healing. In silence that was agony, he waited.

The Lady butted Marissa's shoulder again. With leather-clad fingers moving in slow strokes over the horse's nose, she began again. "When I returned to Argentina to marry Paulo, no one but Juan understood that I needed to stay busy. Like the blind seeking light, or the renegade seeking peace, I needed drudgery. Grinding, grueling labor that punished my body and numbed my mind. He understood that only then could I find an ease for grief that wouldn't go away."

"Were you grieving for us, Marissa?" Jefferson's own gloved hands were fisted to keep them at his side. She was a strong woman, her troubles were her own to bear. Troubles she'd hidden from the world and him. Their last day in the swamp had been the first crack in the dam of hidden emotions. Today was the second rift in that wall.

A small leak in the dam she could deal with. A leak and a stiffened spine were an equal match. Comfort and tenderness could be her undoing. A deluge, with one pent-up emotion tumbling over another, and another, could be too much. Too much, too soon.

Going against every ingrained instinct, but certain he was

right, Jefferson held himself apart. But not aloof. He could never be aloof where Marissa was concerned.

Black Jack whinnied, calling to the horses in the pasture. Drawn to the stallion, The Lady trotted away. Marissa's hand drifted to the splintered railing. As she clutched it, leather served as protection against stabbing splinters of wood.

The land was quiet. Only the stream, cleaving the lull as it cleaved the canyon, raced along its banks, babbling in whispers, catching light in ripples as it went. The canyon would be a canyon without water. But what it brought to the land made it a better place. As loving Jefferson made her a stronger woman. One who could do what she must, for all but herself.

The thought surprised her. She'd never seen her life in that light before. She'd seen only her own shortcomings. Condemned no one but herself for emotions she couldn't control.

"I grieved for both of us. For what we discovered too late and could never have. Then, there was guilt." Turning, with her back to the fence, her body nearly touching his, she looked up at him. Her eyes, normally unfathomable darkness, were spangled with light as they studied the lines of his face. "I spent years wallowing in guilt because I couldn't love Paulo. A good man, a man of old values, guided by old standards. Who with my parents, counted on Marissa Alexandre being the dutiful daughter as they denied her the most important choice a young woman can make. The man she would love and spend her life with.

"You asked me to stay." Tears threatened and were denied. "Like a fool, I didn't."

"Never a fool, sweetheart." Jefferson couldn't let her assume another burden. "You were what you were expected to be. Your father was desperate." He didn't know how desperate a father must be to do what Alexandre had done to Marissa. But it was too late to judge. "You made the choice any caring daughter would make, bearing the brunt of your father's mistaken business ventures and their need to sustain a lifestyle."

The perfect daughter. She'd used the words herself. Subconsciously condemning her shortcomings. What only *she* considered failures. This, Jefferson thought, explained decisions she'd made in the past, and the unwarranted blame.

"You weren't perfect, Marissa. But out of love you made selfless choices. Adams made the same sort of choices and bore the same sort of consequences for me."

Marissa wouldn't look at him. Instead, she stared down at the ground. Freed from its binding ribbon, the fall of her dark hair tumbled over her shoulder, veiling her face. He knew she was wrestling with the sense of what he was saying.

Sliding off his gloves, letting them drop where they would, Jefferson risked a touch. With a bare finger at her chin, he lifted her face to his. "In an act of love, you married a man you didn't love. In another act of love, Adams took the blame for a blow I struck in a brawl I instigated. You both went to a prison of sorts, for someone you care for."

"Marriage to Paulo wasn't a prison, Jefferson." She wouldn't paint the marriage black to excuse herself.

"No?" His finger moved from her chin, skimming the line of her jaw to the sensitive spot at the corner of her mouth. At the slow caress, she shivered, but didn't speak or move away. Years had passed since he'd discovered the wonderful response. But a hundred more could pass before he forgot. "I suspect that if the two of you compared notes, you would find strong similarities. In some ways, Adams's prison offered more freedom."

"Don't make me a martyr. I never suffered in my marriage."

"Perhaps not. But can you deny you were the sacrificial lamb on the altar of riches?"

She was silent. How could one argue with the truth?

Jefferson's knuckles moved over her lower lip, then her chin and the line her throat. Unfurling his fist, he stroked the base, measuring the rush of her heart in the tiny hollow. His voice was deeper when he spoke again. "Adams was deprived of his freedom, and I can never forgive myself for the years my senseless act of bravado and vengeance took from him. But even prison didn't take from Adams what marriage took from you."

Marissa understood, then, what she hadn't thought to consider before. Jefferson was speaking of her body. Of the mating of a husband and wife as expected within marriage. But her marriage to Paulo Rei was never based on normal expectations.

For that she was grateful to Paulo. No matter what else he wanted of her, none of it had been physical. In this bargain, he had been kinder and more generous than she'd expected.

Such a man deserved to be mourned by a celibate wife.

But Jefferson had been kind as well. He deserved the truth. Moving a little, only enough to break physical contact, she admitted what she'd once thought she would never speak of to anyone. "My marriage to Paulo wasn't that sort of arrangement. We were..." With the halting of a confession that would be shocking, she searched for the right words to make this easier. But, she discovered there were no such words. No easy way.

She had never lied to Jefferson. At the same time, she hadn't been as honest as she should have been. It was time he knew the truth. All of it. When her lashes lifted and her eyes sought his, he saw more pain than he'd ever seen before. "Paulo and I were never intimate. Our marriage was never consummated."

Nothing she could have said would have shocked him more. No man in his right mind who was married to a woman like Marissa would be content in a platonic relationship. "That's impossible."

With a shudder, he bit back his doubt. Marissa wouldn't lie about this. Which meant she wouldn't have lied to Paulo Rei either. "You told him about us, and the day in the swamp."

"Yes." She wouldn't equivocate about something as important as what she must tell Jefferson. "All he asked was who my lover had been. Then he confessed that during the time I had spent in Belle Terre, a medical condition caused him to be impotent. There couldn't be the sort of union and the children he'd planned, but he still wanted the marriage. With no recriminations, no demands and only one restriction—that there be no other lovers.

"The greatest surprise of all was that he offered to release me from the agreement completely and he would forgive my father's debt anyway." A shoulder lifted in regret. "But there was the matter of the questions and gossip. Perhaps a scandal I didn't want my mother to face. Then, there was my father's honor."

"Damn his honor!" Jefferson snarled. "What honor is there in any of this? Except yours, when you kept the agreement?"

Marissa's gaze held his, in her pale face, her eyes were bleak. "Haven't you done exactly the same sort of thing for your own father, Jefferson? Haven't you made costly sacrifices in pride and peace of mind for Gus Cade? Don't most children at some time in their lives? Tell me which of your brothers has not."

His anger died on his lips. How could he fault such courage and wisdom? He wouldn't spoil the time they had, brooding about time lost. "You're right. We won't speak of it again."

"Perhaps we should," Marissa began.

Though he wanted to hear the rest of what she had to say more than anything, with a finger at her lips, he stopped the revelation. "Listen. Someone has gotten past the guards."

With that warning, neither moved. In the dusty corral, with only the shuffle of restless horses breaking the quiet, Marissa strained to hear what Jefferson heard. At first, there were only the noises of the ranch. Then she could distinguish the sound of a car or a truck, negotiating the precarious incline into the canyon. Someone who was driving recklessly.

It was the scrape of metal against rock that captured Jefferson's reluctant attention. Reluctant only for that frozen instant. With a second scrape, he was galvanized into action. "Marissa, I want you to go to the barn."

"No." She had no intention of running for cover, leaving him to face whoever and whatever this was alone.

"I'll be fine." He'd caught a glimpse of the vehicle. "I recognize the car. It belongs to a friend. A very close friend, one I trust. But there's no need in taking a chance she's not alone." He turned her toward the barn. "You've only a minute and one more turn before we're visible from the road. Hurry."

Marissa hurried. Jefferson scaled the fence, and went to wait for Cristal Lane in front of the house.

"Hello, handsome." As Jefferson closed the door of Cristal's convertible, she rose on tiptoe to kiss his cheek.

"Hello, yourself, Miss Cristal." With a concerned check of her tires, he leaned against a glossy red fender a layer of dust couldn't dim. "What brings you so far from Silverton?"

"You make it sound as if it's been a long time since I came by to visit." A long red nail traced down his throat to his chest. "When I was here just…" Eyes as green as new, sweet grass laughed up at him. "Well, I was here sometime not so long ago."

"Three months ago," Jefferson supplied. "You were worried because I hadn't been into town in a while. Instead of celebrating your third twenty-ninth birthday with patrons of the saloon, you drove this wicked machine across Benedict land bringing your celebration to me. To find out how I was."

"Oh," Cristal said. "Can't a disreputable saloon keeper spend her own holiday with a friend without ulterior motives?"

"Yes, she can," Jefferson agreed reasonably. "But she shouldn't. Not when there are better opportunities in town."

Slender shoulders moved in an elegant shrug. A coil of windblown auburn hair fell over her cheek. "Maybe I'm not looking for opportunities. If I were, name me one in Silverton."

Jefferson raised an incredulous brow. He could name a half dozen or more. And one in particular, who didn't know yet quite what to think of this supposedly shady lady whose heart was pure, bigger than the world, and twice as tender. "So," he said, "I take it you were worried again."

"Okay." Color flooded Cristal's tawny cheeks, turning green eyes greener. Exasperated that she was so transparent, she threw up her hands. "You got me, handsome. Billy said you'd been home for a visit. I wondered how it went."

"How would you expect it to go?" Billy had done his work well. The surprise was that he'd chosen Cristal, the one person in Silverton least likely to gossip. Especially about Jefferson Cade. "Or did Billy tell you that, too."

"Okay, so Billy Blackhawk didn't tell me anything." Cristal came to lean against the car beside him. "The truth is the great Apache hardly acknowledges me with more than a scowl. You'd think I was the prerequisite fallen woman and he the dedicated sheriff waiting for a reason to run me out of town.''

Jefferson chuckled and ruffled her tousled, auburn mane even more. As the chuckle grew into a laugh, he threw an arm around her shoulders and dropped a kiss on the top of her head. ''Last time I looked Billy was only half Apache and he *was* sheriff of Silverton. I don't think either's due to change anytime soon.''

''Half Apache by blood. All Apache in mind-set. He's hated me since I came to town. Stubborn, too gorgeous for his own good...'' Cristal searched for proper castigation. When it escaped her, she sighed. ''... bullheaded, gorgeous *creature.*''

Jefferson laughed. ''When are you two going to decide what you're going to be when you grow up?''

''Decide?'' Cristal scowled at her favorite friend. ''What's to decide? We hate each other. It's in the genes. The age old clash of the stalwart lawman and the bawdy lady.''

''You're repeating yourself. Same song, second verse.'' He stroked her hair, taming it. ''If you and Billy hate each other, I hope someone hates me as much some day.'' The comment was tongue-in-cheek and utterly serious. ''Not Billy, of course.''

An elbow in his ribs took his breath away. Cristal muttered, ''That was a dumb thing to say.''

''Which part,'' he asked when he could speak again.

''All of it.'' With an exasperated gesture, Cristal raked a hand through her hair, undoing Jefferson's taming.

''Ah. You're that sure, are you?''

''As sure as my name is...well, what it is.''

Jefferson chuckled then. ''Tell me that when you two finally decide if you're going to be friends, foes, or lovers.''

''That's a no brainer. I just finished saying our magnificent Blackhawk has absolutely no use for me. Or I for him.''

''Perhaps the gentleman protests too much. And the lady.''

Cristal stared at him. ''You've gotta be kidding.'' Another look turned into a frown. ''You're not kidding.''

Recognizing a lost cause, Jefferson shifted subjects. ''What I'm doing is wondering what really brought you here.''

''Belle Terre, like I said. Jasper and Billy were talking in the post office about your trip. I eavesdropped.''

''Ah.'' If Billy wanted word of his supposed trip to Belle Terre to filter through the territory, Jasper Hill, veteran postmaster, inveterate gossip, was the one to do it. ''I suppose Jasper decided that's why my mail was accumulating.''

''Actually, he was wondering why your brother, Adams, would be writing you here while you were visiting him there.''

''If Jasper's reading postmarks, he needs more to do.''

''Billy told Jasper he would bring the mail out later this evening. After Billy left, I decided it was time I took an afternoon and evening off to visit my favorite lowlander. So, here I am, Silverton's newest mail deliverer. Or something.''

''So now you've seen I'm in one piece and healthy and you're still lingering. Something else on your mind, Cristal?''

''I'm waiting to be introduced to your lady friend.''

''My what?''

''Your lady friend. The tall brunette who dashed to the barn as I came down the grade. You might also explain the good-looking cowhand patrolling the road by the rim of the canyon. I know all Sandy's men, remember. Almost as well as Sandy.''

"With your hell-for-leather driving, I'm surprised you see anything but dust." He was stalling. Cristal was too sharp and he didn't know how to explain. He chose diversion, while he gathered his thoughts. "How did you get past the new cowhand? Why would you think he's patrolling the canyon rim?"

Cristal's green gaze flashed to Jefferson's, seeking answers in their shuttered depths. "Why else would he stop me, asking what business I had on Benedict range, or the Broken Spur?"

"So, you showed him the mail, claiming to be the carrier."

"Well, yes." Her shoulders lifted again in a "what else could I do?" sort of twitch. "Isn't that what I am, today?"

"Today and the only day," Jefferson observed dryly. "But I see it worked. He let you pass."

"Well," Cristal drawled, hedging more than a little.

"Let me guess, Ethan didn't let you pass."

"Ah, so that was Ethan." Her face brightened. "I'd seen him in town, always going or coming from Billy's office. But then, cowhands are always in and out of there, resolving one problem or another. I didn't know until today that he worked for the Rafter B. I must say the name fits. He certainly looks like an Ethan, all stern and broody. And when he gets here, I suppose, angry."

"In other words, with the accelerator on the floor, you left Ethan in the dust." Jefferson wanted to shake her for being so foolhardy. "You could've been shot."

Cristal's laugh was low and husky. "No one shoots the local bawdy lady, especially when she offers to share the cookies she's brought to a friend."

For the second time in less than a very few minutes, the sound of an engine rent the usual peace of the canyon. "Ah, that's surely Ethan, now." She was smiling in anticipation of a good row with a handsome, dangerous man. "He must've had a vehicle stashed somewhere out of sight. Quicker than a horse, no doubt.

"Why don't you run along to the barn and fetch your guest. Then when Ethan finally makes it down the incline, we can have lemonade and cookies while you both explain."

Jefferson was moving away from Cristal's car, ready to greet another visitor. When he recognized the truck that traveled only a little more carefully than she had, he laughed, though grimly. "I hate to tell you this, Miss Cristal, but I think you're the one who has some explaining to do."

"For visiting an old friend? For bringing cookies? Surely Ethan will understand. Or he will when he takes his first bite." Cristal had come to join Jefferson in the dirt track that served as the road. Now she stopped short as she recognized the truck.

"Oh dear," she muttered. "I don't believe that's Ethan."

"Somehow, I don't either. Not with a star on the door."

"Oh dear," Cristal had time to say again before the truck skidded to a halt. Dust was still billowing like smoke around them, when the door opened, then slammed shut, and a dark-haired, grim-faced golden-eyed giant bore down on them.

"'Oh dear' is right, sweet Cristal." Sarcasm dripped from Billy Blackhawk's greeting. If it could be called a greeting. Stopping before her, with barely a glance or a nod for Jefferson, massive hands fisted on his hips he glared down at her. "Well?"

Billy was known as a man of monumental patience. A man who never seemed to hurry, even when he did. Part Apache and all stoic, he rarely revealed either anger or frustration. Today was obviously an exception. In the rare times he flashed his attractive, but genuine smile, his teeth gleamed in contrast to his naturally dark skin. The dimples that smile revealed were intriguing, at odds with his magnificent, rough-hewn features.

As he stood toe-to-toe with her there was no monumental patience, or any patience at all. There was no smile, no dimples. If he was forever stoic, forever didn't include this day.

Offering her best smile in place of his, one that brought most men to their knees, Cristal looked up and up. From the button in the center of his shirt, to broad shoulders and a stubborn chin, to dark eyes blazing gold fire. What she saw in that beautiful glare made her smile wobble. Obviously Billy Blackhawk wasn't most men. With a touch of bravado and her own hands resting at her own hips, she drawled, "Well, what, Blackhawk?"

"Why the hell are you here?" Billy never cursed. Never.

Jefferson's brows shot up, but he stayed neutral and out of the fray. From where he stood, despite the disparity in size, they were evenly matched opponents.

"You don't curse, Billy, so stop. Gentlemen don't curse a lady. Anyway, it won't intimidate me." As if she would match him in stubbornness if not size, Cristal scowled at the sheriff.

"I didn't think it would. And I do curse when I'm as angry as I am now. Lady or not." Billy's broad hand swept up, powerful fingers threaded through her hair, gathering it at her nape. What could have been a brutal jerk, was a gentle tilt of her head. Golden eyes boring in the depths of her green gaze, his tone turned deadly calm. "I asked what you're doing here, Miss Lane."

"A minute ago, I was Cristal."

"Yeah, well, that was a minute ago. I'm calmer now."

"This is calm?"

"I said calmer. Which, for the moment, means I've decided not to break your beautiful neck."

"In that case may I suggest we all go inside out of the hot sun?" Marissa had come to stand by Jefferson. "Then we can explain some things and make some decisions."

Billy ceased glaring at his nemesis and faced Marissa. His hat was suddenly in his hand, as it hadn't been before. His demeanor was calm, on the surface. "If you're worried this was a grave breach of security, Marissa, don't be."

He directed their attention to the rim of the canyon where Ethan sat, rifle at the ready. Spaced along the only entrance to the canyon, were two more riders. Each with weapons as ready. "By my order, any unidentified intruder who doesn't halt on command, will be fired on.

"One of those riders is a crack-shot called out of retirement. She can shoot an earring from your ear, never drawing blood. Unless she wants to." Rounding on Cristal, the only one who wore earrings, Billy's calm tone vanished. "As for you? You're damned lucky Ethan had seen you in town and recognized you."

Not to be outdone, Cristal tilted her head to meet his gaze. "Is that why you're angry, Blackhawk?" she asked thoughtfully. "Were you afraid I might be shot by mistake?"

"Yes," he growled and took her arm, leading her less than gently to the house. "But only because it would deny me the pleasure of wringing your neck."

"Why, Blackhawk, I didn't know you cared."

"Don't flatter yourself, Cristal Lane."

"Don't worry. I won't."

Following behind them, Jefferson twined his fingers through Marissa's. "Sounds like love."

Marissa's heart was in her eyes. "I hope so. Someday."

"Count on it," he murmured and squeezed her hand.

Seven

No one ate cookies.

With tension and easing tempers still ragged, no one remembered he or she was thirsty. The interior of the house was cooler. If only by a little, at least there was that. With that degree of physical comfort, in this taut moment, Marissa remembered her surprise when she discovered the difference the sliver of shade cast by the near canyon wall could mean.

Once the house had been a cabin, its single room serving as kitchen, living space, and sleeping quarters. With the Cody's addition of a bedroom wing and a second floor, its functions changed. Though still the heart of the house, serving two purposes rather than three should have made it seem more spacious. But in the charged atmosphere, Marissa felt the walls closing in on her.

She suspected the others felt the same. Cristal Lane had taken a chair by the fireplace. Billy Blackhawk stood like

sculpted stone, his back to the mantel, Cristal at his right.
The kitchen table where Marissa sat by Jefferson, on his
left.

The shadow of the vermilion bluff had crept farther
across the canyon floor, enveloping the cabin in an ever
deepening cocoon of dusk. No one thought to turn on a
lamp. No one cared. In dusky light, Marissa considered the
woman across the room. A woman Jefferson had teased as
she'd rarely known him to tease.

It was good to hear the lighthearted exchange. But when
he'd drawn the red-haired beauty into his arms and kissed
the top of her head, envy, even jealousy, had pierced the
watcher's heart.

She'd scolded herself for being a fool and not realizing
that in four years Jefferson would have special friends.
Even lovers. Then the sheriff had arrived, and she'd seen
how it was between Cristal Lane and Billy Blackhawk.

She felt it now, an almost tangible part of all that charged
the air. A cataclysmic emotion that couldn't remain static,
and one day must spill over into hatred or love.

Marissa let her gaze dwell on Cristal who sat so rigid on
the sofa, tangled in things she didn't understand. Then, in
somber, uneasy silence, drawing her gaze from the vibrant
woman only a little older than she, she turned her attention
to the sheriff. Dour, stern, he bore little resemblance to the
Billy Blackhawk who had come to Simon's valley.

His grim mood was due as much to the fact that it was
Cristal who had been involved in today's events as the dis-
tress her rash act had caused. Anyone entering the canyon
as she had would cause concern. But in this case, there was
an extraordinary animosity.

They were like magnets. Billy and Cristal, repelling each
other in personal friction, in turmoil. But turned on the right
track, they would be drawn to each other, more powerfully

than now. Too powerful to resist. Then they would build the enduring bond of strong people. And…lovers?

Unconsciously Marissa sighed and, resting her hands on the table, wound them restlessly over each other. Without word or sound, as naturally as if he'd been doing it forever, Jefferson laid his hand over hers, folding them into his clasp. Turning to meet his gaze, she was warmed by his tender support.

Their relationship in Belle Terre had begun gradually, building from common interests into friendship. Then into love. A voiceless love that deepened into a strength as quiet. It was, in contrast, as gentle as Cristal and Billy's was explosive.

But Marissa knew that if she could get past the doubt that scored her soul, this impasse would resolve itself. When she believed again in what her heart told her, she and Jefferson would find their way as lovers. Then, unencumbered by doubt and grief, the embers of their passion would be incandescent.

Engulfed with the meteoric heat of desire for that day, she turned her hand within his grasp and struggled to find her way to peace, and to him. Fitting her palm to his, slowly her fingers curled, keeping Jefferson the little while she could. Her clasp was desperate, wanting. In a glance she found his gaze riveted on their joined hands. As if he felt the touch of her searching look, his arresting blue regard lifted to her face and to her eyes. When Marissa thought she would lose herself in their brilliant blue, he caught a long trembling breath. A smile, slow and beguiling, shone in their mesmerizing depths.

And her eyes burned with tears for the lost years.

"I suppose there's no help for this."

The words rang in her mind. No help at all, Marissa agreed. Then she gave her attention to Billy Blackhawk, who had spoken the prophetic words.

"It's done and nothing can change what's happened." Billy reiterated a totally different thought. His narrowed eyes flicked from one person to the next, his frown grave. "Cristal has discovered Marissa's here. An unfortunate happenstance, leaving us to make the best of it we can. If you're in agreement, Marissa and Jefferson, it might help her to understand the urgent need for secrecy if she knows why."

"Which brings up another problem." Jefferson's concern was evident to Marissa in the unconscious pressure of his hand over hers. "Every person who knows the circumstances behind Marissa's being at the Broken Spur adds to the danger. Knowledge in this case could be life-threatening. It would be simpler if we asked Cristal for her silence and her word that she won't speak of today. The less she's involved, the safer for all of us."

"Exactly, Jefferson, if Cristal is satisfied with that. If she will promise us her cooperation," Billy agreed. In contrast to his agitated behavior by the corral and his anger with Cristal, he was totally in control. He didn't tug at the cuffs of the perfectly pressed shirt of his immaculate uniform. He didn't rake a turbulent hand through his burnished hair—black as night and drawn back from his forehead to be controlled at his nape by a leather thong. Much as Jefferson had worn his years ago.

Marissa realized Billy Blackhawk wasn't a man given to excessive displays of emotion or wasted motion—except in face-to-face conflict with Cristal Lane. When addressing the threat of danger, he became the consummate professional, cooler and calmer and grimmer with each second.

She hated the subterfuge, the emotional tumult she'd brought into the lives of all she touched. Now the circle was growing.

Lingering tears welled in her eyes, clung to her lashes. She willed them away and refused to look at Jefferson as she felt the weight of his concern. She had to speak, to tell them this couldn't be. That she couldn't allow the risk they were taking.

"Don't, Jefferson. Don't, Billy. I can't do this anymore. Too much has happened, too many people have been hurt or killed because of me. I didn't realize the scope of this, or the effect it might have on any who were involved."

Pausing, she slid her gaze from Billy to Cristal to Jefferson. "I want it to stop, here and now." She'd taken her hand away from Jefferson's. Free, lost without his strength, but determined, her joined fingers clenched in her lap. "At first light tomorrow, I'll leave. Then no one else will be hurt."

Jefferson had sensed this building since she'd stood with him listening to the sound of Cristal's car barreling down the incline. He knew how it felt to be responsible for drawing innocent people into danger. He was well acquainted with the helplessness of watching matters spiral out of control. He understood heartache, and self-inflicted bitterness.

He knew the hurt. He felt it now, in empathy for Marissa, the only woman he'd ever loved. The only woman he could love. Heart aching, he fought a battle with himself, even then he barely resisted reaching out for her. To comfort her, to remind her none of this was her doing. Instead, keeping a careful distance, he asked, "Where would you go, Marissa? What would you do?

"For the love of God, sweetheart, tell me how I live with myself if I let you face something that isn't your fault alone?"

"You can live with yourself, Jefferson, because it has nothing to do with you. You wouldn't have been a part of this if I hadn't—" Marissa's voice broke. The downward sweep of her lashes to hide her emotions revealed how she hated the weakness.

"I wouldn't have been a part of this if you hadn't called

in a promise made long ago on a rare day in the lowcountry,'' Jefferson finished for her. ''But you're wrong, my love.''

''You wouldn't, if I hadn't been weak.'' Cristal and Billy creased to exist for her. There was only Jefferson, and she must make him understand she had to go. ''You're a man who keeps promises. No one knows that better than I. If I hadn't—''

''*If,*'' he interrupted softly. ''The world and life are full of questions. We can always second-guess ourselves with that damning word. *If* I hadn't made the promise. *If* I hadn't loved you. *If* your father hadn't sent you to Belle Terre and Eden. *If* he hadn't given you into Juan's care long before that. *If* Juan hadn't taught you to ride like a gaucho.

''If your father hadn't promised you to Paulo Rei, none of this would have happened. That's the most damning of all.''

Jefferson dared to take her hands, to open her whitened fingers and lace his own through them. As he continued his hushed monologue there was no one else in the room for either of them now. ''How many of that list could you have changed?''

''One.'' Her answer was a whispered breath. ''The one that mattered. The one that drew you into this, Jefferson.''

She looked across the room made welcoming and comfortable by another woman who had to choose between her father and the man she loved. In greater wisdom Savannah Benedict had chosen love over duty. Wisdom a young Marissa hadn't learned.

Marissa's gaze settled on Billy, the giant of a man whose eyes were as black as his hair. Eyes that watched her as he listened, the scowl he had turned on Cristal replaced by a neutral expression. She knew he would never regret helping her, but she regretted the need. ''If I hadn't reached out to you, Jefferson, your life wouldn't be in turmoil. Cristal wouldn't be in danger. Billy wouldn't be worrying over me, over you, over Cristal.

"If I leave, she won't have to be told any more. She can return to Silverton and go on with her life like this day never happened. She'll be safe. All of you will be safe."

"As Jefferson asked, where would you go, little one?" Billy spoke at last. As tall as Marissa was, the name would have been absurd coming from anyone but him. "How will you hide yourself from this man who has informants everywhere?"

"Everywhere, Billy?" she mocked, but her voice was soft.

"Money talks. Even as he hungers for more, the man in question has plenty." Billy still hadn't moved, he hardly seemed to blink an eye. He could stand for hours and not move, not blink. He had. As part of a ritual of his father's people. "What he wants, he takes. What he can't have—" Pausing, as the hard look left his face, he emphasized softly, "What he can't have, he destroys."

Marissa remembered Menendez's sly advances, touches bordering on insult, yet not quite. She remembered the final, lurid proposition. A sickening ultimatum. Menendez was a monster.

"A destroyer." She didn't realize she'd spoken out loud until she found Jefferson and Billy, and Cristal waiting.

"When he couldn't buy Paulo, his business, or his wife—" her lips curled in contempt "—Menendez destroyed him and, he believes, the little toy he lusted after.

"He *believes*." Marissa faced Jefferson. "That's my protection. As long as he's sure he succeeded in silencing us, he won't look for me. No matter his far-reaching influence, no matter his fortune, what he isn't looking for, he can't find."

"And if the plane is found?" Billy asked.

"It won't be." There was still grief in her voice as she assured the sheriff. "It went into the sea."

"Maybe." Billy's gaze held hers. In the first of twilight, his Native American ancestry even more apparent. "That was speculation. It doesn't mean the plane won't be discovered somewhere, someday. By someone."

"Then I'll deal with that when it happens."

"Wherever you are, Marissa?" It was Jefferson who asked. Jefferson who wouldn't keep her from leaving if she insisted. But she wouldn't go alone.

"I'm sure Simon can suggest a reasonably safe place. If not, I can find one myself."

Jefferson didn't ask if she would consider Simon's valley. That question had been irrevocably resolved weeks ago. The questions he asked were much more discouraging. "How will you live, Marissa? What will you do to keep body and soul together? I know you have money of your own. But the first penny you touch, Menendez will know you're alive."

"He'll find you," Billy added, going for the jugular with the truth. "The first indication that someone who has denied him and who poses the greatest threat to his grand plan still walks the earth, the search will begin. He won't stop until he can control you. Or when one of you is dead."

His black eyes holding Marissa's, compelling her to listen, to think, to believe, Billy's voice was grave and very soft when he murmured, "There are some things worse than dying, Marissa. Vicente Menendez is a master at inventing ways to make you wish you had been on that plane."

Fighting back a shudder and tearing her gaze from Billy's, Marissa stared down at the cherry tabletop. "I know what you're trying to do. I know why. Don't think I don't appreciate that you care, Billy. But it changes nothing.

"I have to go." Her head came up, her gaze touched on each of them. Cristal, vibrant and so very alive, but thoughtful and quiet. Billy, grim, concerned, a man of wonderful contrasts.

And Jefferson. Dear Jefferson, more rugged, older and harder now, but still the Prince Charming she'd found in the lowcountry. Her prince, her lover, her only love. She would do what she must to keep him safe. "When I go, foolhardy or wise, I'll have to take whatever consequences come my way. And whatever chances."

"You would risk your life, your freedom, or both for those you care about." It wasn't a question. And for once, Billy's stoicism deserted him.

Marissa didn't respond. Now it was her gaze that held Billy's captive. "Wouldn't you?" She didn't need an answer. He couldn't know she'd read his answer in his eyes when he looked at Cristal. "It seems only fair, doesn't it?"

"When you all get through deciding what's best for everyone, including me, do I get a say in this?" Cristal's serene comment was soothing music in taut silence.

As if with the power of a look he could compel her to understand, Billy didn't look away from Marissa. His voice was a low, impatient growl. "Be quiet, Cristal."

"I will not. I've been quiet long enough. Too long." Before he could rebuke her, she was on her feet, standing before him. Challenging him as if he didn't tower over her. As if one controlling clasp of his huge hands couldn't send her reeling back to her seat. If he should dare. But everyone in the room knew he wouldn't, especially Cristal.

"Why should I be quiet, Blackhawk?" she challenged though her tone was the calm contralto of before. "Tell me why, if you can, when it was my blundering that caused all this."

"Perhaps because two blunders don't make a right," the sheriff suggested.

"Oh, good grief." Cristal groaned. "Don't tell me you've added speaking in fractured clichés to Apache, and an oh-so-perfect English. Perfect for being perfected at Oxford, no less."

As she dropped that little-known bombshell on him, she moved closer, but only to stand before the mantel. Her eyes lifted to the bare wall where Jefferson's painting of a young and beautiful woman had hung when she last visited. The occasion of her third twenty-ninth birthday, as he had reminded her in a lack of gallantry he committed only when he teased.

Cristal realized now the portrait she had admired was a painting of a very young and beautiful Marissa Rei. Except she'd been Marissa Alexandre then. When questioned about the painting and the model, Jefferson said little but that if the painting was beautiful it was because the woman was beautiful. He'd spoken no more of his model except to say she was once a dear friend.

"Very dear." Cristal interpreted the remembrance. But she had suspected even then that the young woman in the painting was far more than a friend, more than dear. Perhaps the woman who had taken his heart when she chose to leave him.

But now the portrait was nowhere in sight, and the woman, who was more than a friend, was back in Jefferson's life. If anyone deserved a second chance, it was this strong but gentle man who would likely love but once.

Turning on the heel of a stylish boot, Cristal stood with her feet apart, bracing for a battle. In a shaft of light falling through a window, she was elegance in black leather pants, black vest, and a russet blouse that made her look as if she belonged on the fashion runway, not in a saloon in Silverton.

Unmindful of the picture she made or that she took a reluctant Goliath's breath away, she regarded each member of her captive audience. When it seemed she wouldn't speak, she broke the unsettling silence. "For once in his life, our illustrious sheriff is right about me. I did blunder into this. I thought I was visiting a friend. The last thing I expected in our quiet cattle country was to walk into the midst of clandestine affairs. The last thing I wanted was to make life difficult for anyone.

"I don't know what this is about. But not knowing doesn't keep me from caring what happens to the people involved."

She cast a look at Billy Blackhawk, green gaze met black and lingered. Cristal was first to look away, but only because she had something that very much needed saying. "I can deduce enough to know that Jefferson and Marissa have a history. Perhaps there was an affair."

She was skirting too closely to personal matters. Billy made a sound and a move as if he would stop her. Cristal ignored him. "But I really think not. Or else neither of you would have allowed the years of separation. I can't know what happened in the interim, except that Marissa lost her husband and her parents. For that, I'm truly sorry. I know, too, that she's in trouble. Trouble that brought Jefferson rushing to the rescue, with Billy not far behind. I know someone called Menendez is involved, and that he's a rich and vicious man.

"Beyond that, I know very little. But I can tell you this, Billy and Jefferson, you both underestimate Marissa." An open palm held up toward Billy stopped the comment he wasn't going to make. "You act as if she's fragile. Grieving? Yes. Carrying unwarranted guilt? I imagine so. But fragile? Never."

Saving the most important for last, Cristal faced Marissa squarely. Her hair was dark fire and her features contoured by pale light and darkness as the day grew older. As she accused, her voice lost its scolding tone. "As for you, young lady."

Marissa waited, silently. Though they'd barely been introduced, and then not officially, an instant bond of respect had leapt between the two women, like the rare meeting of different yet kindred souls. A frisson of jealousy had become respect and she very much wanted to hear what this woman who knew the land and these men far better than she had to say.

Seeing how intently the younger woman watched her, how quietly she waited, Cristal realized that what she said could be the resolving factor. Perhaps her judgment could be the catalyst that decided whether this fugitive from tragedy and menace left the canyon, or if she stayed. If she listened and if she cared half as much as Cristal suspected, Marissa would never leave Jefferson again. "You misjudge us. Billy. Me. Especially Jefferson. Whatever danger you might have brought to the canyon, it would never be more than these men, or even I can handle.

"Maybe neither of us has been through what you have. But we've each had our own losses and our own troubles. Our own trial by fire. We lived through it, we survived. And in the end we became stronger people. So will you, Marissa."

"How can you know that, Cristal? On less than an hour's acquaintance, how can you say what I will be?" Marissa had studied this rare woman, and she'd listened. She speculated that there was the wisdom of misfortune in her words.

"I know you, because I know Jefferson. I know because I know the kind of woman he would be drawn to. The sort it would take to turn him into a brooding loner. Half the single female population of Silverton is in heat for him. Some not so single. None subtly. Yet in four years, he's never been tempted.

"He wouldn't become involved simply for the sake of his masculine or even sexual gratification. And he isn't the sort to settle for a second-best love. He couldn't. He's waited four years for you. And if you think Jefferson Cade could let the woman he loves walk out of his life a second time for any reason but that she doesn't love him in return, lady, you don't know your man.

"Here in the canyon you both have security and the protection of those three riders Billy pointed out to us. And you have Billy, himself. If you leave the Broken Spur, Jefferson will leave with you. He'll go wherever you go, Marissa. Into any danger. I promise you."

Marissa was too stunned by Cristal's blunt assessment to think. She really wanted to look at Jefferson to judge his reaction. But she dared not. Not yet. "I don't want to bring harm to anyone, and I don't want to be a burden."

"Danger is Billy's business and Jefferson won't be lacking when the chips are down. As far as being a burden, or intruding on Billy's time, don't worry. He needs more to do," Cristal asserted. "Then he wouldn't have time to irritate me."

Billy Blackhawk groaned softly, but said nothing. Neither did Jefferson. Cristal was obviously on the right track and neither wanted to interfere.

"As for me," Cristal continued. "I'm stronger than I look. And I'll be all right. Billy might very well like to break my neck himself at times. But he would kill anyone else who tried.

"That's my two cents and change. I can't make up your mind for you. I can't make you stay. But I hope I've given you something to think about. Remember this hasn't been just your loss. It was Jefferson's, too, since the day he lost you. Now that you've found each other, don't waste time grieving over a past not of your making. I hope you'll stay, for Jefferson, and for me."

"For you?" Marissa hadn't expected this.

Cristal laughed. A genuine laugh that lightened the tensions pervading the room. "Hey! I need a friend and an ally. Who wouldn't dealing with these two? Now, I've had my say. I'm out of breath, and I'm heading home. I need to be in Silverton in time to close the saloon."

With a hug for Marissa, a kiss for Jefferson, and a sassy wave for Billy, Cristal was gone. Only seconds after the last of her footsteps sounded on the stairs, the powerful engine of her convertible roared through the canyon.

"Who is she?" Marissa asked as the sound faded. "How did she become so wise?"

"No one knows very much about Cristal." Billy offered the answer. "She arrived in Silverton one day. Liked what she saw and decided to stay. She's a good listener, but she rarely talks much. Today was the most I've heard her say at once in the five years she's been in town. For all any of us know of her past, she might as well have been born the day she arrived in Silverton."

"You've never run a background check?" Jefferson asked, though he knew all he needed to know about Cristal.

"I could," Billy shrugged. "But I won't stoop to invading her privacy without due cause. Despite our conflict, she hasn't given any cause. Now, if you both will excuse me." He reached for his hat, which had rested on the mantel since he entered the house. "I have work to do, and you two have decisions to make. Jefferson, I've a couple of things to discuss, if you'll walk with me to the car."

Sundown had long passed. Ruby cliffs turned to deep purple, then utter black. Long shadows casting puddles of darkness over the canyon had been swallowed by the night. A silver moon rode low in the sky and from the pasture a night bird called.

The supper no one wanted was done and Marissa sat on

the top step of the porch, with only Satan as her companion. The massive Doberman was given to wandering away for small chunks of time, but he always wandered back. Always to Marissa. He seemed to sense when she needed him and when she didn't. Tonight he lay as close as he could get, his head rested on her thigh as he slept.

This should have been a pleasant time, a time of accomplishment for one who had reveled in the long hours in the saddle herding the canyon horses to home pasture. But as she stroked Satan's head, Marissa could think of nothing but what Cristal had said.

"Then, lady, you don't know your man," she whispered the last of the most stunning statements.

"She's right, you know." Jefferson stood at the bottom of the steps, watching her in the moonlight.

After supper, with the untouched food put away and the kitchen in order, while Marissa excused herself to go upstairs to soak her aches, he'd gone to the barn to check the horses close to foaling. For one this would be the first foal and the mare was restless and frightened. Marissa hadn't offered to help for she needed to think. And no one was better at soothing a skittish horse than Jefferson.

"I didn't hear your footsteps." She looked down at him. Now that the sun had gone and he no longer needed the protection of his hat, his head was bare. Though his hair was wet and darkened, streaks of silver still gleamed in moonlight. His shirt was open, his belt unbuckled. She knew then he'd bathed in the creek. The vision of how he would look standing naked in water reflecting a thousand moons sent shards of desire spiraling through her.

Suddenly insecure and uncertain, she said the first thing that came to mind. "You cut your hair."

Jefferson didn't smile at the inane remark. "A long time ago. But so did you."

His face was in shadow as he looked up at her, but she

knew his intense blue eyes were watching every nuance of every expression. "It was easier shorter."

"Yes."

Her hand stopped stroking Satan. Her eyes strained to read what was in his face. But there was nothing she could distinguish. Drawing a long breath, she whispered, "Is it true?"

Jefferson didn't pretend that he didn't understand what she was asking. "It's true."

"You've waited all these years for me?"

His head inclined a bare inch. "Until I heard from you again, I didn't realize I was waiting. But, yes, I have."

"You won't let me walk out of your life a second time?"

"Only when it's safe, and if you don't love me." His hand was on the banister, but he made no move to climb the steps to her.

"In return?" Marissa stared down at the lean shape he projected in the dark. "Cristal said in return."

"I love you, Marissa. I have for longer than you know."

It was simple declaration. And more beautiful for its simplicity. There were tears in her eyes, but this time she didn't blink them away. "Four years is a long time to wait."

"I would wait longer. Forever, if need be."

"If I ask you not to leave the ranch, would you stay?"

"Not if you go."

Clasping her hands at her shoulders, hugging herself, she murmured, "Even if I don't love you?"

"Even then," he admitted, adding softly, "But you do love me, Marissa. I saw it on the plain. I saw it by the lake in Simon's valley. I've seen it here. I'm a part of every breath you take, every beat of your heart. As you are in mine."

Her tears spilled at last, leaving tracks of wonder on her face. "If I stay?" she whispered hoarsely. "What happens then?"

"What do you want, love? Tell me and I'll try my best to make it happen. I'll do whatever it takes to make you happy."

Marissa made a sound that was almost laughter. "You make me happy just by being Jefferson."

That small sound released him from his self-imposed restraints. With agile grace he climbed the steps to sit beside her. Gathering her in his arms, with only the lightest of kisses brushed across her forehead, careful not to go faster and further than she was ready to deal with, he held her. And together they watched the night.

Neither knew how long they sat in the darkness. Neither cared. But after a time, she relaxed, curling into him. Breathing a sigh of longing, she murmured his name. And Jefferson stood, his arm outstretched as he whispered unforgotten words from the past. "Take my hand, sweetheart. If you truly want this. If you truly want me."

Marissa's trembling fingers met Jefferson's strong clasp. Satan whimpered, but slept on as his master swept the woman for whom he'd waited a lifetime into his tender embrace.

Eight

Hands joined, fingers twined with Jefferson's, Marissa walked with him through the house. She wore a long, loose dress of a thousand tiny pleats reaching from shoulders to toes. A gift from Raven that had quickly become a favorite in those evenings she normally spent in her room after a soothing bath.

But tonight, the walls of her room had also seemed to close in on her, driving her from its confines. To the porch, to the night. To Jefferson.

The pressure of his clasp drew her to a halt, spinning her to face him, setting the thousand pleats rippling about her. Catching her free hand, then drawing both to his lips, between small kisses trailed over her knuckles, he whispered, "Did I tell you how beautiful you are tonight?"

"Am I?" Was it vain, she wondered, to want to hear him say the words? To revel in them. Treasure them.

"Since the first day I saw you." Opening her fingers one

by one, he linked them around his neck. Drawing her body to his, he smiled down at her. "My brothers, Lincoln and Jackson, and I had come to Eden's Inn. And there you were, just coming from the garden. Your long hair wild and tangled from the wind, a basket of flowers in your arms.

"Over what seemed like blossoms of every sort found in the lowcountry, and of every color, you looked at me like some enchanted creature. I'd never seen anyone like you. Or felt for anyone what I felt for you."

"I didn't know. I didn't understand. Not then."

"You weren't supposed to know, sweetheart. I was eight years older and you had your whole life ahead of you. Though not the life I expected. But that's the past." Slowly, with her arms still linked at his nape, and his at her waist, he began to move in the smooth, gliding steps of a waltz. "Do you realize that in all those years, we never danced together? I never held you in my arms, until it was too late."

"It isn't too late now," she murmured, and leaned her head against his shoulder, giving herself up to the silent music guiding his steps. As naturally as if they'd always danced together, her body matched the tempo of his.

In moonlight falling through a window, bodies close, hearts keeping time, Jefferson danced with his love to strains of music only they could hear.

After a time, his steps slowed, his lips traced over the satin skin of her temples, then her ear. Softly, on a breath, he asked, "What do you want, sweetheart?"

Her head came up, her eyes met his. "I want you, Jefferson. I want forever. However long forever can be."

"Yes," Jefferson agreed hoarsely. A single word that said everything. Then he was lifting her into his arms, striding to his bedroom. A single lamp burned by his bed. In its pool of light he set her on her feet.

When she swayed against him, he made a desperate

sound and bent to kiss her with the hunger of years. His mouth was gentle and demanding, devouring and giving at once. As her lips parted, his kiss deepened. His tongue caressed hers. His hands spanned her waist, urging her closer.

Marissa's fingers glided up the column of his neck, damp strands of his hair threaded through her fingers as she cupped her palms around the back of his head. She wanted to keep his mouth, his kiss, his intimate caress. She couldn't drink deeply enough of him. Or get close enough.

His long, lean body was her bulwark. Her support. Her haven in the storm.

He made her whole.

Curling her fingers, catching fists of his hair, she drew him away. Denying herself what she wanted most, to say what she must. "Jefferson," she whispered as he looked down at her, a look she couldn't fathom on his face. His eyes, catching the little light, held the question he didn't voice.

"I'm sorry." A tremor sounded in her soft words.

She was so close, every nuance of her breathless words seemed to flow over him like a touch. Two words that would set the course of his life. Keeping her in his embrace, he asked gently, "What is it, sweetheart?"

"I'm sorry for the years. For the hurt. I'm sorry for so many things." Bowing her head, she touched her forehead to his shoulder again. As she caught that ever-familiar calming breath, her breasts touching his chest, she shivered, returning her gaze to his. "I'm sorry I didn't have the wisdom and strength of Savannah Cody, or the vision of Cristal Lane."

"And now?" Jefferson's palms skimmed slowly over her ribs, then her back, coming to rest at the curve of her shoulders. His splayed fingers touched her nape, her hair, her throat. His thumbs strayed over the line of her jaw to the corners of her mouth. Her lips, when he traced their shape, were still moist from his kiss. "Are you sorry now? For this?"

Marissa's look moved over his face, touching every feature, seeing the strength, the love. "Only for the lost days, the lost hours, the minutes."

"The seconds," he finished for her as his mouth took hers in another kiss, and another, as with his tender touch he made her forget about sorrow. About grief. "Time doesn't matter tonight. Tomorrow's a new day, a new start, a new life."

"Together," she whispered softly against his throat as she stepped from the circle of his arms. The slender column of her dress swayed as she moved. The ripple of pleats molded her body and danced around her ankles. With a shake of her head her hair tumbled down her back.

Jefferson had only a second to realize that as her breath came in uneven shivers her unfettered breasts strained against the pleats. Then, with the graceful crossing of her arms and the stroke of her palms, the dress was gliding from her shoulders and her arms, baring her body inch by glorious inch.

When the supple garment lay in a forgotten pool at her feet, she didn't speak. She didn't move. Marissa, an entrancing woman. A woman who knew what she wanted, and believed at last there was no guilt in the wanting.

Jefferson's body shook, his chest rose and fell in harsh, uneven rhythms. His eyes never wavering from her, he shrugged from his shirt, kicked aside his boots. As quickly the rest of his clothing followed.

He was fiercely aroused and he wanted her, needed her desperately. But not yet. Despite the heavy throbbing demand, he wanted to claim her first with his eyes and his touch. As a blind man who must see with his fingertips, he traced the line of her brow, the contour of her cheek, lingered long at the pulsing, fragrant hollow of her throat.

Then his quest moved lower, discovering her breasts were a perfect fit for his cupped palms. As he cradled them gently and leaned to taste first one taut nipple, then the other, his gentle suckling was rewarded with her quaking sigh. Her body swayed and the sigh became a low cry as his questing caress trailed over her midriff to her waist. Then down her hips to clasp her buttocks as he had her breasts, drawing her to him, at last.

She was beautiful, as beautiful as in his memory. She was tawny grace and long, lean elegance. A temptress, an awakening wanton. A mystery to unravel again and again. A treasure to hold, to keep, to protect. Forever.

Then she reached for him to work her own sweet magic. Setting his heart pounding in a wild erratic rhythm, she was the siren whose silent song was her touch. A touch that left nothing undiscovered, nothing unworshiped. In the space of a shivering gasp, he was beset by torture that was as artless as it was provocative. As beguiled as it was beguiling. A madness drawing him ever deeper into the storm.

She was wonder and agony that had him crying, "Enough. Dear heaven! Enough."

Then he was sweeping her into his arms to take her, at last, to his bed. A bed that once had known the passion of other lovers, yet in his time had been solitary—but no more. Even as he regretted laying her on a bachelor's utilitarian counterpane when she should have silks, he knew she must understand this couldn't be just one night. Or two, or even a dozen.

Not once he made love to her. For when he did, he knew he couldn't let her go a second time.

Brushing her hair from her face, he stood looking down at her. "I've dreamed of this." His voice was hoarse, strained, as he struggled for the last of his control. "I want you more than anything. More than life. But only for forever.

"Tell me now, Marissa. Tell me what you want. Say the words. I need to hear the words."

Lying so quiet with her taut, shallow breath hardly a ripple in the stillness, she met his look. As he had kissed her and caressed her, in a smoky whisper he had called her beautiful over and over. But he was the one of true beauty. Rugged, masculine, virile beauty. His face less pretty and more handsome with age.

His body had grown leaner and harder and strong. His features bore the mark of sun and wind. But he had weathered the onslaught well. The frown lines, the crinkles and creases only served to make him more intriguing. The darkening of his skin defined the power of brawny muscles. Hours in the saddle kept his stomach flat, his hips lean, and corded his thighs with muscles.

He was a man who had chosen to live in a harsh, unforgiving land, yet had never succumbed to the harshness.

He was all she hoped. "Forever isn't long enough."

"No?" he asked, his voice rough with need.

"Not nearly." She laughed softly as she took his hand. "But if you promise to love me as I love you every day of forever? Then forever's a promise I'll take, and give in return."

"So will I." Jefferson smiled as he came down to her. And as his body joined with hers, as the ease of heartache began in the healing of love, into the enchanting fragrance of her hair he murmured, "Forever, indeed, my heart."

Long into the night he made love to her and she to him. Sometimes with whispered words. Sometimes with wandering caresses and gliding kisses. Sometimes in the raw and intimate hunger of joined bodies, gleaming with the sheen of the sweat of exertion, seeking to be closer, deeper.

Kindling again and again the flames that licked at them until the firestorm swept them over the edge into mind-shattering rapture.

Just before dawn, they fell silent and still. Too weary to do more than whisper the last of countless words of love. Too weary to move, it was in a lovers' embrace that sleep claimed them.

At dawn, Marissa rose, plucked her dress from the floor and tiptoed from the room. When she stepped onto the porch and into the cool predawn air, she slipped on the dress and sank to the top step to watch the canyon wake. There was light on the horizon, turning the sky and the canyon walls astonishing colors, long before the sun truly rose.

Marissa didn't know how long she'd sat without moving, falling in love with the canyon all over again, when Jefferson's footsteps sounded behind her. Even as she looked up, he was bending down to sit beside her. His chest and arms were naked, and only jeans covered his lower body.

"Mornin', darlin,'" he drawled in his best Southern accent. "I missed you when I woke up. Then I decided that maybe you were running for cover."

Smiling, Marissa didn't rise to the teasing challenge. "Never running. Only enjoying the morning."

Jefferson's palm at her chin turned her face to him. His blue gaze studied her carefully, looking for any hurt he might have inflicted with a passion that, in retrospect, seemed too strong even to him. "Don't play games, sweetheart. Did I hurt you? When I was thinking straight again, I was afraid…"

Marissa's hand came up between their bodies, her fingers folded over his mouth, stopping his words. "Last night was beautiful, not painful. Loving me could never hurt." She smiled then. "I'm a little tired, pleasantly achy, and I've never felt so wonderful in my life."

He laughed then, a low sexy chuckle. His fingers slipped from her face to her hair, ruffling it as he planted a chaste kiss on her forehead. He couldn't really kiss her. Not if he meant to keep from tumbling her back on the porch and taking her again.

"Too tired to take Gitano and Black Jack for a ride later?" His fingers left her tousled hair to skim over her lips. If he couldn't kiss her, at least he could touch her. "I have a surprise for you."

"A surprise?" Her breath came in short, little gasps as the touch of his fingertips on her tender lips sent sensations racing to the most achy part of her body.

"Don't ask, for if I tell you, it won't be a surprise." Rising from the porch, he held out his hand. "In the meantime, how about a swim and a bath in the stream?"

"A swim?" Marissa couldn't remember anywhere the stream was more than hip or waist deep.

"There's a place beyond the pasture where the creek is fed by a small waterfall. For electricity, Steve put in a small generator and harnessed the power of the fall. Then, he did some excavating, adding irrigation and landscaping to create a small lake as a special gift to Savannah."

In her weeks in the canyon, Marissa had never had any inkling there was more water than the two streams she'd seen. "Is that where you bathed last night?"

"No." The barest move of his head accompanied his denial. "I was saving the lake for a special occasion. This one."

Giving him her hand as her assent, she rose to stand beside him. "How do we go? Walk? Horseback?"

"Neither, my love." Jefferson was laughing as he tugged her down the steps. "We go by the cowboy's second-best steed."

"The truck," Marissa supplied. Then, her gaze raking down his body, she wondered out loud, "If we're both going as we are, it should be interesting if more unexpected visitors arrive.''

"Doesn't matter." His grin teased. "If anyone dares intrude, I'll just have Satan eat them."

"Right."

Then there was no time for more and he dragged her to the truck. The pleated dress swirled and danced around her legs while the supple fabric played touch and tell, teasing the sensitive points of her breasts. When he helped her into the truck and climbed in beside her, she knew he should've looked ridiculous dressed in only jeans and Stetson. But the truth was he looked like nothing but what he was, magnificent, sexy, and all male.

"Ready when you are," he said, his fingers hovering over the key already inserted in the ignition.

Marissa knew he was giving her one more chance to back away. One last chance to avoid the lovemaking that would be an inevitable part of their interlude by the lake. "I'm ready now."

The drive was slow, uneven, a wonderful adventure. Marissa saw a different view of the canyon. At first sight, from the rim, it had appeared cloistered, closed in by the very walls that protected it. From the floor, the canyon was a veritable mix of ecosystems. Her first look at the waterfall that fell an incredible distance into a small cul-de-sac, and she realized she had seen it all along. But from the distance of the house and barn, she had never recognized it as a fall, assuming it was another quirk in striations of rock walls that were constantly unique.

When Jefferson brought the truck to a halt, he waited a minute to let her take in the wonder Steve had created for his wife. "Amazing, isn't it?"

"More than amazing." Marissa looked from palms to

ferns tucked in shady alcoves, to brilliant tropical flowers. "But no more amazing than Sunrise Canyon, itself."

"The secret is water, sweetheart. Men have been known to kill for it in this land." Gripping the steering wheel, he turned from her. "That was a part of why Jake Benedict coveted the canyon for most of his life. Likely he still does. Even though it belongs to his daughter and her husband. Offer a man gold or good water out here and only a fool would take gold."

"Steve Cody was no fool," she ventured. "But how did a down-on-his-luck rodeo man come to have it at all?"

"It was a gift. Steve saved a friend's life at the risk of his own. A fellow rodeo man and an old nemesis of Jake's who had better things to do than battle the old man."

Marissa heard respect in the name. *Old man.* "You like him. Jake Benedict, I mean."

"I do." Jefferson's attention seemed to be riveted on the tumbling fall of water, yet his mind was on the past, when he was a young runaway looking for a home. "He can be a son of a bitch. But he goes after what he wants fairly. As Savannah did."

"Savannah wanted Steve?"

Jefferson laughed. "Eventually." Opening the door, he crossed to Marissa. When she stood beside him, he said, "Despite the temperature, the water will be cold. A lot of dynamics figure into the reason, but I like Savannah's best."

"Which is?" Marissa was beginning to realize how fond Jefferson was of Savannah Cody, as well. She hoped someday she would meet and know the legendary woman.

"She thinks, quite simply, the water outraces the sun."

"And, therefore, is never warmed by it."

Jefferson nodded, turning to her. "Ready to skinny-dip?"

* * *

The water was as cold as he'd warned, but invigorating. Even restful. Later, sitting on a grassy bank covered by a bath sheet Jefferson had taken from his truck, Marissa soaked in the heat, finding peace in a manmade desert oasis. A gift of love. A secret trysting place for that love.

Jefferson sat beside her, a towel draped at his waist. "Nobody intrudes. Which isn't surprising since few people know it's here. This was Savannah's place. Steve wanted her to have the freedom to do whatever she wished here."

"Like this?" With a turn of her face and a tilt of her head, she touched her lips to his shoulder. With the lave of her tongue, she felt the heat of the sun on his skin and the clean, exciting taste of him. When he went still and tense, she laughed wickedly, letting her breath cool the moisture left on his shoulder by her tongue.

In a swift move he turned to her, his hands at her shoulders bearing her down on the velvet of the sheet. A low growl rumbled in his throat as he muttered, "Or this."

Then his hands and lips were everywhere. Stroking, petting, seeking out new, maddening, undiscovered responses of her body. Adding them to the old, blending old with the new. Sending sensation after sensation rocketing through her.

Jefferson's long legs tangled with hers. Using their muscular power he turned, lifting her high above him. Then gradually he lowered her to him. There was a fierceness in her now. And she was sweet and hot as she took him, riding him like the Cossack she'd been named. Wanting even more, she leaned over him, her fingers in his hair, her breasts a caress of their own against the hard plain of his chest.

When the first nuance of release fluttered through her, with incredible strength he surged upward, matching her rhythm with powerful thrusts. When she cried out, in his own final passion he gathered her to him and held her through the euphoria.

In the return of serenity, as she fit so perfectly in his arms, he found peace he'd never expected to know again. She was the light in his darkness. Perhaps his way back to all he'd lost.

Then, with one hand tangled in the spill of her hair, the other flung across her body as if he would watch over her and keep her forever, Jefferson drowsed in the heat of the day. When he felt her relax in the abandonment of sleep, he slept as well.

"Wake up, sleeping beauty." Jefferson leaned over her, loving the way she woke. Quickly, completely, but with a dreamy, remembering look in her eyes.

"Jefferson." As she looked up at him, she touched his face, her palm cupping his cheek, her fingers curling at the tender skin at his temple. "Good morning."

"It was, wasn't it?" He laughed softly and kissed the tip of her nose.

"Was?" Her fingers slipped into his hair, loving the shining blend of silver and deep gold.

"Nearly." He tilted his head to kiss the tender line of her wrist. "It's almost noon."

"Then we have hungry horses."

"No, Sandy Gannon has seen to them. I spoke with him about it last night." There was no one Jefferson trusted more than the foreman of Jake Benedict's Rafter B. He would trust Sandy with his life. And if all else failed, with Marissa's.

She laughed, suddenly. She'd forgotten the nearly un-used telephones in the house and the tack room of the barn. "You planned this, and here I was thinking it was spontaneous."

"Let's just say, I hoped." Leaning closer, kissing her

eyes, her nose, then lingering at her mouth, he murmured against her lips, "Any complaints?"

Marissa's answer was to tug at his hair, bringing his kiss closer, deeper. When she let him move away, the laughter in her eyes was enticing. "Does that answer your question?"

"Oh yeah." He grinned down at her, savoring the easy camaraderie of lovers who, for one short and passionate interlude, lived together in a world apart. "If I had the stamina, I would show you exactly how much. But alas."

When he left the rest for her to remember, she laughed again and ruffled his hair. "Poor baby."

A look he couldn't fathom flickered over her face. It came, then was controlled so quickly, he would have missed it if he hadn't been watching closely. In a dreaded moment he feared it was grief and unmerited guilt for loving him in every sense. "Hey, sweetheart, what is it?"

"It's nothing." A minute shake of her head accompanied the denial. As she saw his need to be assured she had accepted the past as something she couldn't change, and that her grief for her parents, for Paulo, was finally without guilt, she smiled. "It truly is nothing, Jefferson. Except, maybe I'm a little sad that days this wonderful were so long coming for us."

"They're here now, to stay. And each will only get better," he promised. "As soon as—" Breaking off, because he didn't want to sully this place and this morning with the name of danger, greed and murder, he changed the subject. "I have another surprise, if you're up to another ride. This time on horseback."

"Black Jack and Gitano," Marissa recalled.

"Want to try? It won't hurt the young horses to have the day off, and Sandy has seen to the rest of our chores. While we're gone the riders on the rim will watch over the ranch."

"We're riding out of the canyon?"

"Yeah." He grinned again. "There's something I want to show you."

"Another lake?" she drawled.

Rising to his feet, he scooped up his towel and secured it around his waist again. Then, he turned, his hand reaching out to her, waiting for hers. "Not another lake," he assured as he drew her up and back into his embrace for a quick kiss. "But something I think you'll like even better."

As the crow flies, the trip would have been much shorter. There was even another faster, more direct route. Because Jefferson didn't want to tax Marissa any more, so she wouldn't be staggering from fatigue, he led her across easier terrain. Along the way, he pointed out interesting rock formations, birds and animals, and plants. Especially the cacti. A common thing in Arizona, a rarity on the plains of Argentina. Finally at the rim of a low bluff, he reined Gitano to a halt.

Leaning on the pommel of his saddle, he smiled as Marissa came to join him. With a wave of his hand, he offered his surprise. "As promised. Today and weeks ago."

Below the rim, a little distance away, a weathered cabin sat at the far end in a small cul-de-sac. There were two corrals. One attached to a barn as weathered as the house. Another by a trickle of a stream. There were no animals, no people. Yet on this hot day, smoke drifted from the chimney. Someone cooked.

Marissa turned from the scene below, her eyes sparkled. "Jake Benedict's newest acquisition." It wasn't a question and she didn't wait for an answer. "Juan, Marta, and Alejandro. They're here."

"Two days ago. One to travel in, one to settle down." Seeing her so happy twice in one day made it a great day for him. "Shall we ride down, say howdy and welcome to Arizona?"

"Yes. But first, thank you."

Shifting in the saddle, Marissa reached across Jefferson. Clasping a hand at his nape, she brought him down to her kiss. Her lips were soft, giving, sweet. If this was gratitude, he knew he could never have enough of it.

When she moved away, he knew the kiss had had the same effect on her. "You know something, sweetheart," he began in a roughened voice. "This bonfire of ours is turning into an eternal flame."

"Would you have it any other way, my love?"

"No," he admitted when he could breathe again. She had never called him anything but Jefferson, and in rare times, Jeffie. The endearment, spoken in sudden gravity, added to the hope that burned in his heart. "Never any other way."

Jefferson touched her face, his eyes filled with desire. Then he remembered that people who were special to her waited for this day as eagerly as she had. He satisfied himself with a feather light tap on her lips. The promise of other kisses. Then, smiling, he gathered up his reins. "Shall we ride, my love?"

"She looks happy." Juan didn't smile, but there was relief in his voice.

"She is." Jefferson didn't look away from the small house, or from Marissa. She sat on the steps with Marta. Alejandro sat in her lap, chattering, gesturing, more animated than he'd seen the child. Neither she nor the boy had let each other go from the moment she'd rode into the yard to hail the house.

Though their conversation didn't carry to the barn or the corral where Jefferson stood with Juan, their laughter did. The trill of the boy's happy giggle blending with Marissa's contralto with such regularity, made it clear the reunion was a joyful return of old habits. In what once would have seemed to him to be rare exuberance, Marta was clearly expounding on this new home. A home she could never have expected before.

But for all the elation in this time, it was Marissa who held Jefferson's exclusive attention. Marissa and Alejandro.

This small, handsome child with his dark, dark hair and eyes as dark could've been her child. And, as she bent to kiss his cheek, or ruffle his hair, laughingly accepted another of many hugs, only a blind man wouldn't see that the love was as strong.

Tearing his gaze from her, he spoke to Juan. "Marissa has worried about you. Knowing you're all safe and close is the best of it." With a thumb, Jefferson tilted back the brim of his hat. His sky-blue eyes returned again to the woman and child. "Especially Alejandro."

"There is a special bond between them," Juan agreed. "There was no doctor when he was born. Just Rissa. He wasn't positioned properly for the birth. In the greatest patience and with only what she'd learned in the stables, she turned the infant. For me, it was a miracle."

The gaucho's hands closed tightly over a splintered rail. "If not for Rissa, I would have lost them both."

Jefferson nodded. He could understand, for he'd witnessed her skill at River Trace, his brother's horse farm. If the fates were kind, he would witness it again on the Broken Spur.

If they were kinder still, one day she would have children of her own. His sons, his daughters. No, he amended, our sons, our daughters.

He hadn't let himself think that far into the future before. But standing in the heat and dust, hearing her laugh, seeing the love on her face as she held a child, Jefferson knew he wanted a life and a family with Marissa.

A life, a family, and forever.

Nine

"Tired?"

Marissa didn't lift her chin from her folded hands, or turn from the darkening and ever fascinating sunset. Regretting the concern she heard in Jefferson's deep voice, she answered, honestly, "Of course." Then to ease his mind she smiled her assurance. "But pleasantly so."

Quiet returned to the porch again. Only Satan, sleeping by her side, scratched at the wooden floor as he chased some elusive creature in his dreams. For once hardly aware of the dog's antics, from her place on the top step Marissa watched the end of day in continued preoccupied silence.

Jefferson stood only a pace away, hipshot, shoulder braced against a post. He was oblivious of the time or the canyon and the shadows that crept across its walls. His attention and his world revolved around the woman huddled at his feet.

Riding back from the Elias's new home, she had grown

quieter. The joy of the day had been replaced by a mantle of melancholy. He assumed it was the sadness of saying goodbye to her friends, even for a little while. A grief he thought would ease. But the rest of the day and evening had been no different.

Supper was another fiasco that neither of them wanted. Now she'd sat for nearly an hour, silent and brooding. Whatever it was that had sent her into this mood, he had to understand. To help, if he could. Sitting down beside her, with an arm around her shoulder, he asked, "Are you thinking about Alejandro?"

Nodding and lifting both hands, with the heel of her palms, she squeezed her temples as if she would push her thoughts away. In a continuation of that same motion, with her fingers she combed her hair back from her face, before clasping her hands again as tightly as before.

The clean scent of her surrounded him, tantalized him, as strands of her falling hair brushed the back of his wrist. Hair that smelled of sunlight. Dark hair, as dark as the boy's.

It was strange that since he'd seen them together again, all thoughts seemed to lead to the black-eyed child. Marissa's thoughts, as well, he suspected. "He's on your mind even more now that he's close. It's obvious how much you love him."

She didn't speak for a while. Easing the clasp of her hands, reaching across her body, she laced her fingers through his. "I think of him. Constantly. I always have. But tonight is different. Tonight Alejandro is a reminder of something I should tell you. Something I should have told you long ago."

Jefferson felt the sudden clench of premonition in his gut. The grip of his fingers over hers was unconsciously fierce. "Then now is as good a time as any, isn't it?"

"As good as any?" she whispered hoarsely. "I don't

know. But it's the best time we have now.'' Turning in his embrace, her solemn gaze held his. Her breasts rose and fell in one long, unsteady breath. ''There was a baby, Jefferson. Our baby, conceived that last day in the tree house.''

Pausing she waited for his reaction. Anger, disgust, regret, anything. When there was none, when he sat as still as death, waiting, she continued her revelation in a somber, lifeless tone. ''When I knew, I went to Paulo again. This time, he released me from our final agreement and all my promises. I was making arrangements to come back to you. Then, for no apparent medical reason, it was over. Too soon to know if our child would be a boy or a girl, it was gone.''

''Then there was no reason to come home to me.'' Though he spoke of things other than the child, the hurt, the loss, colored his voice. In his tone there was the grief of unspoken words.

Sliding her hand from his, she framed his face between her fingers. ''There was always reason, my love. But—''

''*But,*'' Jefferson interrupted with a grimace. ''*If.* There's always one or the other, isn't there?''

''For us, so it would seem.'' She wanted to hold him and comfort him, but the look in his eyes, the tension in his face, warned it was too little, too late.

''What was it this time? No.'' With an abrupt, humorless laugh he stopped any explanation she might make. ''Let me guess. Does it go something like this…the discovery that you were expecting the child of another man, a stranger, caused such a furor your mother became even more ill.

''So ill that when our baby was lost, you had to stay. To be the dutiful daughter again,'' he finished, bitterly. Bitter for her, never with her. For he understood how the Alexandres worked. Understanding their sort and their selfishness wasn't difficult. Even without knowing them. "All for that precious lifestyle that was your price to pay."

Marissa hoped that someday she could make Jefferson understand what was abhorrent to him was an accepted practice among the people who moved in her parents' social and economic circle. She hoped he would know and believe that they thought the arrangement they made had given her the best of her world. In time, perhaps, he would, but not now. Not yet. She need not waste time or breath trying until he was ready to understand.

"My mother's heart problem had taken a severe toll on her in my absence from home. Before I realized I was carrying your child, news of the wedding was widespread. She was really too frail to cope with the scandal of a broken betrothal."

"But she would have had no choice but to cope, if the baby hadn't miscarried? Is that what you're saying, Marissa?" His face was still grim. His voice roughened by pain.

Marissa looked away, gathering her composure. When she turned back to him, there were tears in her eyes and on her cheeks. "I loved my mother. But in choosing a life, my choice would have been our child and you."

Groaning softly, Jefferson reached for her. "I know, sweetheart. I could never doubt that."

Folding her closer, with her head on his shoulder and her face nestled against his throat, he embraced her. Even now, he could feel the pain thrumming in her. Not for the first time, he realized how strong she'd become. The choices she'd had to make were enough to bring the strongest to their knees.

But not Marissa Alexandre.

She had walked out of his life a young woman of clear but untried principles. She had returned to him a woman tested by grief and tragedy. A woman who would walk by his side in the worst and the best of times. A woman to treasure. To love.

For the gift of that woman, Jefferson could even forgive the Alexandres for the time she had been taken from him.

"The baby, our baby, is part of the reason you studied medicine and obstetrics." His fingers glided over her hair, smoothing it. His touch was comforting in the absence of anger.

"I wanted to keep what happened to me from happening to others."

"Juan says you have already. With Alejandro's birth."

"That was good fortune. It was too early in my studies for any real medical knowledge to come to bear. Fortune and dire determination Marta wouldn't lose her child as I had."

She had found her way through grief with strength and a goal. He believed now her mood was a reaction to the resurrection of memories. Memories provoked by a dark-haired child.

"Alejandro is a bit more than three?" he ventured.

She had relaxed beneath his soothing touch and tensed a little again at his question. "Only a bit. If our son or daughter had been meant to be, he or she would be the same age."

"She," he insisted. "I prefer to imagine our baby was a little girl as pretty as her mother."

Leaning away from him, solemnly Marissa searched his face. "You aren't angry that I didn't tell you before?"

"There's nothing to be angry for, sweetheart. All I feel is sorrow for what we've missed." With the pad of his thumb he wiped away the spill of her tears. "And regret that our lost baby never knew what a generous and wonderful woman her mother is."

A low cry sounded in her throat. In the last of twilight,

her eyes were luminous. "You really mean that, don't you?"

"I've never doubted it. Not even when I was struggling to forget you. The more I struggled, the more I proved it couldn't be done. You were—you are—unforgettable."

"And when I reached out to you?"

"I knew I was a goner." As he kissed her cheek, his breath was warm against her skin. "I don't know how your letter found me, but I'll be eternally grateful it did."

She laughed for the first time in hours. "That part was easy. My final letter came to you from Eden. The original packet was a series of letters within letters. With the exception of their separate instructions, I asked that each send it intact to the next person. When it came to Eden, I asked only that she send it to you if she was certain you would want to hear from me."

"And my beloved, first sister-in-law knew I would."

"Perhaps, if she'd known what I was asking, what I was drawing you into, she wouldn't have sent it on."

"She would have. But I'm glad she didn't know. I'm glad none of your helpers know. You took a chance trusting that they would each do what you asked."

"They were good friends, and my only avenue. There was no other choice."

"Then it's truly all's well that ends well?"

"If it ever ends. If we can ever lead normal lives again. If those who have helped me here can have their lives back." Her face was suddenly bleak when she looked to the rim of the canyon. "What are they thinking now, the riders who stand guard? Are they missing their families? Someone special they love? Where do they sleep? When do they sleep?"

"Jake Benedict has a line shack nearby. A step above what you would see in movies, but still a shack. They're accustomed to rough quarters. Even Valentina, I imagine.

Billy's plan was that they would work in overlapping shifts at night. That way one would sleep while two patrolled. But, I figure they're as familiar with catnaps as with rough quarters.''

"Rough quarters, little sleep, away from home and family. I have to wonder, Jefferson, what I ever did to deserve such care. And how long can it go on?''

"You deserve it because every citizen deserves protection. It can go on as long as needed. But Menendez will make a mistake sooner or later, and Simon and his men will have him.''

"I've wondered how Juan and Marta's disappearance was handled. Surely someone questioned how they could be there one day, and gone the next.''

"Ah, sweetheart, never underestimate Simon. A wonderful job opportunity arose for Juan. So wonderful time was of the essence. So wonderful Juan sent a crew to the *estancia* to collect his belongings and make his goodbyes.''

"You think that story will be believed?''

"After seeing Simon in action, do you doubt that he will see to it that it's taken as gospel?''

Marissa smiled then. "Not really. In fact, there were times I had trouble remembering he isn't Superman in disguise. Or that he isn't infallible.''

"Maybe not. But he's as close to both as possible.''

Her short trill of laughter held the sound of conflicting emotions. Abandoning this digression, she spoke again of what was in her heart. "I've wondered how you would feel, what you would say when I told you about the baby. I imagined every reaction.''

"And?'' With the back of his finger he drew a caress from her forehead to the tip of her nose, then to her lips and her throat. The gentle exploration ending at last at the cleft of her breasts just visible within the opening of her shirt.

"I've discovered I love you more than I thought I could." Her voice was husky, her eyes languorous, in response to his intimate quest. "Far more."

"Enough to stay with me when this is done and be my love?"

"I would be your love, your mate, your everything, Jefferson. And stay as long as you want me."

"Then I want forever. And babies. Especially a dark-haired, dark-eyed little girl who looks exactly like her mother."

It was a dream. She was too happy. Happiness this extraordinary couldn't last. But she could pretend for Jefferson. "A boy first," she whispered as she touched her lips to his. "Every girl should have an older brother."

"To keep the wolves from her door." Gathering her to him, he scattered kisses over her face. "A brother to keep her safe, as Juan kept you safe, until a lover comes along."

"As you came for me, Jefferson."

"About those babies, sweetheart. Considering that I wasn't exactly prepared for making love, and considering our track record, we might have made another baby already." He had never asked about birth control. For a faithful woman with an elderly husband in name only, there was no reason.

"How would you feel if there was another baby so soon?" Her expression was a mix of hope and anxiety.

"Like this." Touching her only with his lips, he trailed kisses over her forehead then down the first of the path his plundering finger had taken. One kiss, then another skimmed over her arching eyebrows. "And this." Kisses closed her eyes, and with the tip of his tongue he caught the last of tears shimmering on her lashes. "And just in case we haven't already succeeded, this."

His mouth, when it touched hers at last, was gentle, sweetly seductive, moving again and again over the line of her lips. Teasing, but making no effort to be more. Until, at the end of her restraint, it was she who clasped his nape to keep him, her mouth opening to his in silent need for more. As the intoxicating magic of his response spun through her like delicious flames, she sighed in mournful regret as he drew away.

"There's a better place for this, sweet Marissa."

"This?" She saw the teasing in the quirk of his lips, but knew that with the teasing, he was serious.

"Making love. Making a life with you. Making a baby."

"Is that truly what you want, Jefferson?"

"It's what I truly want, in that order." His smile faded. "If Menendez finds us?"

"He won't." Jefferson willed it to be true.

"But if he should, and it goes bad?"

"Then we will have had this much."

Then he was rising to stand over her. His callused hand reaching down, waiting for her. The instant her hand touched his, he brought her up to him. Up for one more kiss, one more caress before he walked with her to his bedroom.

Jefferson was up first the next morning. Though exhausted and mindless from the night, he had willed himself to wake early. A skill he'd perfected years ago in the wilds of the lowcountry. He was dressed and had just begun planning Marissa's surprise when the rumble of Satan's rare bark reverberated over the yard, then was lost in the thunder of galloping horses.

He was reaching for the rifle he kept loaded and ready by the door when he recognized a familiar voice quieting Satan. An insistent rap pierced the predawn darkness and Juan Elia called for him. Wary of a trick, Jefferson flicked off the light. Easing back a shutter, he peered at the porch and into the yard.

In light of a moon half as bright as day, he saw Juan by the door. Ethan Garrett and Valentina Courtenay, Simon's crack shot called from retirement, stood by their mounts. As he moved to the door, Marissa stepped from the bedroom, dressed and wary.

"Who is it?" There was no panic, only alarm in her voice.

"Juan, with two of the guards from the rim." Jefferson was terse, his gaze holding hers a second before he opened the door. No one thought of greetings as Juan moved past him to Marissa. Moving as quickly, the rim riders were close behind.

"He has him. Menendez has Alejandro. I don't know how, but he does," Juan blurted without preamble, his eyes black holes in a colorless face. "Alejandro wanted to ride with me to check the fences," he explained before anyone asked. "When Marta went to wake him for breakfast, the window was open and he was gone."

A crumpled scrap of paper fluttered from Juan's fist to the table. "This was on his bed."

"A ransom note," Ethan Garrett supplied, familiar with the circumstance. "Menendez will trade the boy for Marissa."

As pale as Juan, Marissa reached out to take his hand, struggling to stay calm. "How long ago did this happen?"

Valentina crossed to Marissa, laying a comforting hand on her shoulder. Though she was much smaller, no one who watched how she moved, or saw the look in her eyes would think her smaller stature indicated lack of strength or ability. "Marta found the boy was missing a little more than an hour ago.

"Wisely, Juan drove the ranch truck as far as he could. Then he switched to horseback when the terrain was impassable for the truck, saving time. Rick and I intercepted him at the last mesa. This was our first inkling of trouble, but we'll find the boy. I give you my word." With a tilt of her head, she met Juan's black gaze. "Both of you."

"You saw no one else?" Marissa asked.

"No, I'm sorry. All we have to go on is the note. But we'll find more." Though Valentina's words were infinitely gentle, they rang with assurance. "Juan and I rode ahead, Ethan came to take his shift and joined us along the way. Rick will be here shortly with Marta. Then we can pool our thoughts and make plans."

The last of Valentina's speech was lost in the jangle of the telephone in the bedroom. The room was eerily quiet. All eyes turned to Jefferson when he reappeared in the doorway.

"Simon," Valentina suggested. "And madder than hell."

"Simon." Jefferson acknowledged. "With an informant's tip and a warning that Menendez is on the move. Madder than hell that it's too late doesn't touch it."

"What's the word?" Ethan asked. "How did this happen? Who knew where Juan and Marta were?" His golden-brown eyes turned to Marissa. "How did he know he could get to you through the Elias?"

"For that matter, how did Menendez know Marissa is alive?" Even worried for his son, Juan was concerned for her.

"Simon's sources report Rei's plane went down in a ravine, virtually intact. Rather than the sea," Jefferson explained. "Proving the theory it was shot down or sabotaged. Not a bomb. One of Menendez's suspected informants found the aircraft. He could've known for days Marissa wasn't on board."

"Which put him days ahead of Simon, giving him time to use Juan to find me. But how did he know about Juan at all?"

"There's a little girl on your family's *estancia*." Jefferson spoke directly to Marissa, dreading what he must tell her. "Her mother brought the girl to you for treatment at the same time Alejandro was ill. The little girl is missing the tip of a finger now. It would have been more if the mother hadn't talked."

"Maria. Her name is Maria. She was a playmate of Alejandro's," Juan supplied hoarsely. "If Menendez would mutilate a three-year-old girl, what will he do to my son?"

"Nothing," Valentina declared vehemently. "Because we're moving on it at first light. We're going to track this animal down and neutralize him before he knows what hit him."

"The note says he will contact us by noon. Instructing where to meet to exchange Marissa for Alejandro." Juan crumpled his hat in his hand, his face stark. "If we make a misstep…"

"We won't." Valentina snatched the note from the table. Crushing the paper in her fist, she tossed it aside.

Jefferson saw in her eyes that she knew Menendez would never let any of the Elias live. But there was one chance. "How do we know this is Menendez? Perhaps he sent his men, but didn't come himself. With Simon on his trail, it would be dangerous for him to enter the country at all."

"Menendez will be there." Ethan had said little. When he spoke, his rage was glacial and that much more ominous. "He likes to inflict his revenge in person. Marissa refused him. He won't tolerate refusal."

"You don't think he intends to let Alejandro go," Marissa spoke so softly her question was barely audible, "do you, Ethan?"

Ethan didn't respond at once. Silence sweeping through the room like a cold wind, was answer enough. After a time, he shrugged. "I wish I could tell you differently, but I've seen his handiwork too many times."

"Ethan's knowledge of Menendez is one reason he was

assigned to this case. And why we're going to jump in first.''

"How do we get that jump, sweet Valentine?" Rick Cahill drawled the fond name as he stood at the door with Marta by his side. In the tension, no one noticed their arrival. Now, with a word and a squeeze at her shoulder, he freed Marta's riveted concentration, sending her into Juan's arms.

"We have the edge in Ethan who knows how Menendez thinks. Added to it there's Billy Blackhawk's word that we have one of the best trackers in Arizona in Jefferson."

"Speaking of Billy, where is he?" Rick asked.

"He's on his way. Simon called him before he called here." Jefferson briefly caressed Marissa's shoulder. "He and his deputies will stay with Marta, and Juan, and Marissa."

"I'm going with you," Marissa stated as a matter of fact. Her tone said implicitly she wouldn't be left behind.

Jefferson still tried. "Sweetheart, you can't."

"Yes, Jefferson I can. I will. Our best bet could be to negotiate with Menendez. Without me, what is there to negotiate?"

"No." He was adamant. "There must be another way."

"She's right, Jefferson." Valentina resolved the argument. "Don't underestimate your lady. She's done well so far. She'll do well in this."

Considering the matter settled, Valentina turned to other concerns. Addressing each with an assurance that left little doubt that she'd done this before. Jefferson remembered a comment Yancey had made. *One of Simon's own—a lady sharpshooter, to be exact—rescued Patrick McCallum's daughter.*

Yancey's words reverberated in his mind. Cold comfort now that the situation was real to him. But he looked at

Valentina Courtenay with renewed respect, and with gratitude for setting retirement aside to come to Marissa's aid.

"All right," he muttered but only to himself. For he knew Marissa's decision was irrevocable. Standing together they listened to Valentina's plan.

Keeping low to the ground, Jefferson dodged by the Elias's ranch buildings and fences, then disappeared into an outcropping of rock. He was dressed in leather the color of the land. His hat had been replaced by a band around his forehead to catch the sweat. His boots, set aside for quieter moccasins.

He blended so well with the terrain and moved so quietly, he stepped on the small mesa before anyone knew he had returned.

"Well?" Valentina wasted no time seeking his report. No one listened more intently as he described what he'd found. When he finished, she was silent, mulling over what he'd said. "You think there were only three of them?"

"Menendez and his two bodyguards," Ethan suggested. "He doesn't go anywhere without them."

"There were only three, and they were headed toward an old mine shaft on the far boundary of the property. Not many people know or remember it's there," Jefferson said grimly.

"Which would suggest Menendez had inside information." Valentina's gaze strafed over the men she worked with. "Any suggestions on the informant?" With an abrupt gesture, she set her question aside. "We can deal with that later. For now, Alejandro is our first priority. Marissa? If we need you?"

"I'm ready. For anything, for Alejandro."

"I expected as much." Turning a look at Jefferson, Valentina smiled and reminded him again, "She's your lady, and worthy of you. As you are of her."

Turning to Ethan and Rick, she said, "Let's get this guy. For Marissa's family. For Alejandro. For Simon. And for all the kids who might someday take drugs brought to this country by Menendez."

Jefferson wasn't wrong. Neither was Ethan. At more than two hours before the noon contact, Menendez and his two bodyguards were hunkered in the little shade provided by the rotten framework of the ancient shaft.

The heat would be horrendous. A fact that made Jefferson more fearful of Menendez. A man of his power had to be eaten alive by the bitter need for revenge to endure such conditions.

"Are you sure about this, Valentina?" he asked.

She was assembling her rifle. When she looked up, her steady gaze met Jefferson's. In that moment he knew he'd never seen a woman as cool, as calm. Until he looked at Marissa.

Valentina's confidence was contagious, and Marissa had absorbed her share. She understood her part in this, and what she must do. Jefferson didn't know he'd shivered until Valentina gripped his arm.

"Jefferson, doubt makes for mistakes. We can't afford either. If we don't believe this can be done, we shouldn't try at all. If one doubts, we all fail." Snapping the rifle case shut, taking up the weapon again, she looked at him. "What will it be?"

"We do this," Marissa answered. "There's no other way."

Jefferson wanted to keep her from the risk she would take. Instead he stood taut with worry.

"I love you, Jefferson." Not caring who heard, she stroked his face. "I want a life with you. A life free of worry, and most of all from guilt. I want babies like Alejandro. I want him to grow up with them. To be an older brother. None of that can be if we don't do this.''

"You aren't afraid to do this, my love?''

"Yes. But I'm more afraid not to do it.''

Jefferson nodded that he understood, because he couldn't speak the words. And he'd never loved her more.

Marissa's fingers slipped from his face to his hair. Drawing him down to her, she whispered against his lips. "Kiss me for luck, and let's get this done.''

With a groan, Jefferson drew her closer. His kiss was desperate, as if with the power of his love he could keep her safe. As harsh as it was, it was the sweetest kiss he'd ever known.

She stepped away, their hands clasped a second longer. "Whatever happens, take care of Alejandro. Promise me that.''

"With my life.'' Because the child was more than Juan and Marta's son, because he was the embodiment of the child she lost, Jefferson vowed she wouldn't lose him again.

When he turned, Rick and Ethan were no longer on the mesa. He knew they'd gone to take up their post. Rigid and unmoving, he watched as Marissa climbed down to her assigned place.

Then there was only Valentina. Everything hinged on her.

"Make it count, Valentina.''

"I intend to, Jefferson.''

"You're pretty confident.''

Her eyes held his. "There can be no doubt in what I do.''

"Have you ever missed?''

Grief scored her face briefly, then was gone. "Once.''

"Why?''

As before, her eyes met his. "A split second of doubt.''

"What happened?"

"In my hesitation, the man I loved took a bullet."

"But you got the shooter."

"I got him."

"The man you loved, what happened?"

"He died, in my arms." There was pain in her voice. "I won't hesitate today, Jefferson. I won't miss. And nobody's going to die. At least, none of us."

She said no more, and too many agonizing minutes to count later, Jefferson was in place. Moving like a ghost, he sprawled in heated dust above the mine shaft. He could see no one. That Ethan and Rick were in place he had to trust to their expertise.

That Valentina could see what she must and could do what she must he trusted to God and Simon.

A child whimpered, a frightened, pitiful sound carrying over the expanse between the mesa and the mine shaft. Then Marissa appeared, calling Menendez's name, taunting him.

A tall, dark man stepped into the open with Alejandro in his arms. Vicente Menendez with a pistol at the boy's head.

Ethan called out from the side of the shaft as planned. Menendez began to shift instinctively toward him, then froze, suspecting a trap. In the second that followed, in sequences too rapid to register except after the fact, all hell broke loose.

A shadow, where no shadow should be, vaulted from a ledge toward Marissa. In tandem, a single shot reverberated through the stillness. A second that could have been its echo whined in ricochet after ricochet. Marissa falling beneath the shadow was the last thing Jefferson saw as he leapt into chaos.

As quickly as it began, the furor ended. The land was still again. The quiet broken only by a child's cry.

Ten

There was laughter in the ranch house of the Broken Spur. Laughter and celebration, for Juan and Marta Elias's son had been returned to them. Still a little clingy, a little frightened and confused, but unharmed and truly safe at last in his mother's arms.

A reason for celebration and laughter. But as he sat at the kitchen table with the others, a heavy weight bore down on Jefferson, sucking the laughter from him. Dampening the elation.

While the others talked, questioned, theorized, he sat solemnly, listening. A part of the team in body. Detached in mind.

Valentina's shot had been true, as she promised. And as she promised, none of them had died. Except Menendez.

His bodyguards had been disabled and by now were under arrest. For, on a signal from Valentina, the second phase of the plan had been set into motion. With Juan and Marta

Elia no longer needing protection, Billy had left the ranch for the mine shaft.

Without the intimidation of their leader, Menendez's men were talking loud and long, telling however much about his singular operation anyone wanted to know. As a sheriff who had fought against drugs all his life, Billy wanted to hear chorus and verse of their revelations while memories of the price of Menendez's crimes was still vividly etched on their minds.

In the flush of success, no one thought past returning Alejandro to his mother. Which Marissa had done a while before. In that time, Alejandro had been bathed and redressed in clothing Marta had brought, to have something of Alejandro's with her.

Now, as the boy sat in Marta's lap stealing shy smiles at him, Jefferson knew their part had ended. Except for the explanations and the rehashing. Jefferson wasn't sure he wanted any part of revisiting all that happened at the shaft. Not when memories of Marissa falling and the whining scream of an endlessly ricocheting bullet ambushed his thoughts at every turn.

But as he heard the questions and saw the need to know written on Juan and Marta's faces, he knew reliving that awful time was inevitable. And as Valentina began to speak, he understood it was an exorcism of sorts for the parents.

"Juan, Marta, Marissa and Jefferson." Valentina looked at each of them before continuing. "Though bringing Alejandro home to you was our chief purpose, we've done more today than save a child. We've toppled what could have become the largest illegal drug operation in the country. We did it by taking a single man out of the equation. For Menendez was a one-man operation."

Jefferson was startled to hear Valentina speak the conclusions he'd drawn from watching Menendez in action, and from hearing the babble of his henchmen. Given her skill, her unique understanding of the people involved and of the situation, he could almost believe she had plucked his thoughts from his mind.

If she had, it wouldn't surprise him. Valentina Courtenay was an intuitive woman. From the time of Juan's arrival, once she heard his frantic revelation, she'd taken charge. Anticipating every move, down to the last detail. Even Marissa's part.

Marissa. He fought back a shudder as his gaze found her with Satan at her side. Satan, who had disobeyed him for the first time since he was a pup. Ignoring a command to stay at the ranch, trailing behind in hiding. With that rare sense of animals, becoming the shadow in the melee at the mine. Her shadow every minute since. As she stroked the Doberman, and in the celebration, the risk she'd taken was forgotten. But never by Jefferson.

Feeling the force of his stare, taking her hand from Satan and abandoning her regard of the Elia family together again, she met his gaze with luminous eyes. As her attention strayed over his features, carefully, cataloging his hurts, sensing his malaise, her expression grew tender.

Jefferson saw the tenderness, he saw the love, but his heart was too encased in ice to respond. If beauty was only in the eye of the beholder, in his eyes she was the most beautiful woman in the world. The first darkening of a long bruise reaching from her forehead, down her temple, to her cheek—a mark of her courage—made her more than beautiful.

Yet he couldn't return her smile. Even as he ached to touch her, he couldn't reach across the table to take her hand.

He could only replay the memory of his paralytic horror at the sound of the wild shot taken by one of Menendez's bodyguards.

Beyond that gut-wrenching moment of despair for Marissa, he had little memory of what he'd seen or done. His body became a mindless machine, doing what it must. He barely recalled that he'd leapt into the midst of the ambush and in one continuous motion had snatched Alejandro from Menendez. Even as the drug czar was collapsing against him, Jefferson wasn't aware of the blood.

It was only a nightmare, until Alejandro locked tiny arms around his neck and buried his tear-streaked face in his throat.

"How?" he asked when all seated at the table fell silent. "How did this happen? With Simon's care and his planning, aside from little Maria and her mother, how could Menendez find Juan and Marta? Who was the informant?

"This should have been foolproof." Suddenly furious, he pushed back his chair and stood, not caring that the chair banged against the wall, scarring the wood. "What damned good were all our precautions when Menendez saw through them like gauze?"

"Call it bad luck or fate, but what happened was the same thing that comes into play in most screw-ups," Valentina answered calmly. "We don't know what went wrong, Jefferson. But I suspect the one thing we can't control, a chance encounter. Perhaps something as innocent as an offhand remark to the wrong person at the wrong time."

"If it was a chance remark, what would it matter?" Marta asked, struggling with the reason behind what happened to her son.

"It matters," Valentina explained, "because of the ramifications. It can be like a stone thrown in a pond. The ripples that radiate from it can affect so many things."

Everyone was quiet. Perhaps thinking how this stone in this pond had changed lives as Valentina continued. "We've seen this sort of innocent mischance ruin covert operations before. We've seen it expose secrets."

Grimacing, she looked up at Jefferson. "We've questioned what we could have done differently each time."

"The answer, in the case of fate, chance, whatever you choose to call it," Marissa observed, directing her response to Jefferson's barely contained anger. "Is nothing."

"Marissa's right," Valentina agreed. "We could put a man from the Florida Keys in the wilds of Idaho, give him a new name, a new occupation, a new life where no one knew him. Then one day, one year, or ten years later, an old friend, an acquaintance, or a stranger who recognizes him could cross his path. And the danger he faced before will be as real as if the years in between had never happened."

Marta who had spoken little throughout the day, spoke again. "What mischance caused Menendez to seek us out and take Alejandro?" Once he was returned to her, she'd been content to hold the boy, to whisper to him as he clung to her. Now, she held him closer. "How could this place that seemed so safe be discovered so easily?"

"I don't know, Marta. We may never know," Valentina answered. "But be assured finding out will be our first priority."

Jefferson couldn't listen to any more. He couldn't stay closed in any longer. Snatching his hat from a hook by the door, he faced them. "Juan, Marta, I'm sorry this happened to Alejandro. I'm glad he's all right. But if you will excuse me, I need to see to the horses."

Turning, he opened the door. When Satan stood, obviously torn between his master and Marissa, Jefferson muttered, "Stay."

Stalking grimly away to the barn, he left a startled silence behind him.

He was working in the barn, finishing the last of a number of unnecessary, time-consuming, grueling chores when he felt her hand on his shoulder. Straightening from his task, his body taut, he tilted his head to stare at the ceiling and the loft. His chest rose and fell in uneven breaths as he heard Marissa call his name.

"Jefferson? Are you all right?" Worry trembled in her voice. "You left so abruptly I was concerned."

"That Menendez's men had injured me?" He wondered how she could worry about him when she had been the decoy. The target of one of Menendez's men in Jefferson Cade's wavering moment.

"Of course I worried," she admitted.

He faced her, his expression bleak as she stepped back. "I'm not hiding any hurt. I wasn't injured." He opened his left hand, revealing a nearly healed cut. "Not even this."

"Then what's wrong?" To assure herself he wasn't making light of some difficulty, she let her gaze rove over him and found only the haunted sadness she'd seen so many times before.

Though he had been working when she entered the barn with Satan at her heels, she recognized it as busy work for a troubled mind. The horses had long since been tended. Because his hair was still damp and he'd changed into the extra set of clothing he kept in the tack room, she knew he'd recently bathed in the stream.

Yet his mood hadn't changed. Jefferson was spoiling for a fight with someone. And that someone seemed to be himself.

"Juan and Marta have taken Alejandro home." She spoke casually, as if the Elias had only come for a visit. "Valentina took them in the truck. Then she'll touch base with Billy. Once this last is settled, she, Rick, and Ethan will be leaving."

He listened, as he watched her. She wore the pleated dress and her hair lay in damp disarray around her shoulders. The shampoo and soap Raven Canfield made of wildflowers rose from it in an intoxicating scent that made him want to kiss her. To learn for himself if the taste was as maddening as the fragrance.

Marissa was all he'd ever wanted. The only woman he'd ever needed. Now the bruise across her temple reminded him with sickening clarity that he'd almost lost her to the ricochet of a bullet.

Beneath his vivid stare and in his silence, Marissa continued as normally as possible. "All that's left are legalities. Valentina thinks we could be called to testify when the bodyguards come to trial. But who knows where or how long that will be. So, we're virtually free, Jefferson."

"Free?" He said the word as if it were a gift and a curse.

"Free to do what we want. To go where we want. Never looking over our shoulder."

"Will you go back to Argentina?"

The question astonished her. Where she might go wouldn't matter as much as with whom. "I'd like to go back. In fact I should, to make arrangements about the *estancia* and other family holdings. But only if you go with me."

"I can't go." There was no inflection in his tone. No life in his eyes. With the back of his hand he traced the purple line of the bruise that marred her face. "I have a way of failing the people I love. First my brother Adams, who spent years in prison for my mistake. Then, in the disgrace, my father. Now you."

Catching his fingers, fitting her palm to his, she kept their joined hands against her cheek. "You've never failed me."

"I made a mistake today. There was a moment…"

"We *all* had a moment. You, me. Rick, Ethan. Do you think Valentina made her shot without her own moment? Not doubt or anything that kept us from doing our part. Just that small second of thinking, what if?" Marissa took a step closer. Not close enough to touch him, but enough to make him stifle a groan. "What you did was save a child, Jefferson."

She kissed the backs of his fingers. "A child—and me."

His eyes closed. The scene playing eternally in his mind, Jefferson turned away. Back straight, shoulders taut, he stared through the barn door that led to the corral and the pasture. On a day that had wreaked havoc with all he believed of himself, bringing disorder to a finally ordered life, the canyon survived.

Through thousands of years, and countless changes, through cataclysm and in quiet times the land continued. The sun was setting. It would rise tomorrow.

As this day ended another would begin. Bringing with it the future. His future, to make of it what he would. If this new fear of the pain of loving and losing didn't cripple him. "Then," he muttered softly, "I lose either way."

A rustle of pleats stirred sweet memories, and the scent of wildflowers surrounded him only a faltering heartbeat before Marissa's gliding caress moved over his back.

A loving touch, worth all the pain and heartache time and fate would require of him.

"Jefferson." Slipping her arms around his waist, she rested her cheek against his broad back. "What is it? What troubles you? Let me help."

Then he was embracing her, holding her as if he would never let her go. His eyes were brilliant, the haunting shadows fading. His smile was tender and pensive at once as he hugged her to him so urgently all her breath was swept from her. His lips were pressed against her hair as he muttered, "I was afraid today. I wanted it to be me facing Menendez, but I knew it couldn't be. Not for Alejandro's sake. My mind knew you had to be the one, but my heart wouldn't listen. And I was so afraid it hurt. Dear God, how it hurt. Sacrificing my own life would have been easier than watching you walk toward that monster.

"Until today I didn't know loving could hurt so much. I keep hearing the bullet and seeing you fall, and God help me, I've never felt so helpless in my life. If it weren't for Satan..."

"Shh." With her fingertips she stopped the deluge. "My love, I know what it's like to watch the person who is your life go into danger. I know how frightening it is. And I know the greater the love, the greater the hurt." Stroking the line of his jaw, she cupped his cheek in her palm. Her dark gaze met his, holding him captive, daring him not to listen and believe. "But hurting doesn't stop us from loving. Not if it's real."

He wondered how he could ever deserve her. "Loving might tear out my heart. It might drive me mad. But it doesn't stop being love, does it?"

"Not unless we let it." Marissa's arms crept around his neck. "Your bedroom has a beautiful view of the canyon. The sun will be setting soon. Have you ever made love there at sunset?"

"Not yet." He laughed softly, a beautiful sound that was far too rare. "An oversight that can be corrected. If my lady's willing."

"Oh, she's willing. On the condition that we forget today, and file it away as a part of loving and growing stronger."

"Stronger," Jefferson repeated, knowing this day had been a lesson in strength, taught by Marissa.

With a kiss he took her in his arms. With another, he murmured, "But there's one more condition. A condition of my own."

"Anything," Marissa declared. "Because I trust you—with my life and with the lives of all I love."

"In that case, sweetheart, you've just agreed to marry me, to be my strength and my love for all time."

"No." She shook her head slowly. "Not agreed. Promised."

"And you always keep a promise."

"Always." With eyes closed she savored the rhythm of his stride. The stride that would take her to the bedroom where they would explore the marvelous, mysterious thing called love.

Early the next morning Jefferson was finishing the surprise he'd planned for Marissa, when the telephone in the bedroom rang. He'd stepped back to view his handiwork, when his bedroom door opened and Marissa appeared with Satan at her side.

"That was Billy." Sweeping her tousled hair from her face, with her back to the fireplace, she faced Jefferson. "The mystery of how Menendez found us has been unraveled."

"By Simon or Billy?" he asked.

"Actually, it was Cristal."

"Billy doesn't talk to Cristal if he can help it. Yell, yes," Jefferson amended. "Talk? Never."

"In whatever volume, the mystery's unraveled."

"Unravel it some more." Jefferson led her to the table, poured cups of coffee, then sat down. "Tell me."

"It was word of mouth, but considering all that followed, it can only be true."

"So?" Jefferson prompted, worrying the handle of his cup.

"Just before Paulo and my parents were to board the plane, the pilot asked for a mechanic to check a tire. Later that mechanic would remember there were only three passengers. He recalled overhearing that I was to join them later."

"Where did he recall this? To whom?" Jefferson wondered how something seen and heard in Argentina could lead to Arizona.

"He chose to talk in a bar, after there were rumors the plane had been found in a ravine. Perhaps he was drunk, or feeling boastful, but he added his gossip to the rest. Who knows who heard, or who repeated it. Our bad luck was that someone along the way was connected to Menendez."

"Makes sense," Jefferson agreed. The situation didn't seem so ludicrous in this light. "Any information brought to Menendez would be pursued by the bodyguards."

"Since I had disappeared, yet was not on the plane, the next logical step would be to look for me at my family's *estancia*." Marissa's expression grew somber. "From there the path led to Juan and his family. Our friendship was never a secret.

"Five minutes on the *estancia* and anyone might speak of our relationship. Because of the connection to Alejandro, Maria's mother would be targeted for questioning. Now, because of me, little Maria is missing part of a finger."

"That still leaves a gap between Argentina and Arizona, sweetheart. Perhaps you could explain it as Billy told it."

"I'm sure you know Billy had been trying to ferret out a drug ring with suspected contacts between the border and Silverton. It isn't inconceivable that the contact here was one of Menendez's men. A man familiar with the territory and the old mine."

"This is where Cristal comes in." Jefferson was a step ahead, but he wanted to hear it spelled out.

"Shortly after her visit to the Broken Spur, Cristal heard one of Billy's off-duty deputies talking out of turn. A new man on the force, trying to impress a lady. Cristal shut him up. Not because she understood the danger in what he was saying, but because she knew Billy Blackhawk's deputies were never to discuss business of any kind outside the office.

"Sadly, she didn't stop it before the deputy bragged about seeing the new folks from Argentina shopping in the feed store and hinting at a mystery involving them."

Jefferson pushed his cup away in disgust. "No doubt that bit of news went straight to one of Menendez's lackeys, too. Then, to Menendez himself. If only Cristal had known to speak up sooner. But there was no reason for her to think it was more than a harmless indiscretion."

"Regrettably, it wasn't until Billy brought Menendez's body and his men to town, and she heard what had happened to Alejandro that she realized the deputy's remark could have some bearing on case."

"Then Valentina was more right than we could know," Jefferson suggested. "A chance remark, or a chance encounter can undermine the most carefully laid plans."

"It could happen to anyone. This time it was us." Regret scored Marissa's face. "I couldn't stop what happened to Alejandro. But now that I'm wiser, I'll do everything I can to make sure it doesn't happen again. Neither to Alejandro, or Maria. I can't restore what she's lost. But I can make it up to her by ensuring her safety and giving her a better place to live.

"The *estancia* is mine. I can claim it now. With your help, I can make a difference in the lives of children like Maria."

"What about Juan and Marta, and Alejandro?" he asked.

"For selfish reasons, I hope they stay in this country. But if they return to Argentina, a share of the *estancia* will be theirs and, one day, Alejandro's."

"What about us, Marissa? Where will we be years from now?"

"I don't care, Jefferson, so long as we're together. If I have that, what else could I want?"

"Let me show you what I want." Offering his hand he

stood, waiting. When she rose, a puzzled look on her face, he led her to the fireplace. "I want that."

Marissa's gaze lifted to the mantel and the painting of a young girl on the edge of womanhood. A portrait of her, that even she could see had been painted through the eyes of love.

"When?" she murmured when she could find her voice.

"I put it up this morning. You were too distracted by Billy's call to notice."

"No, no." Her fingers tightened over his. "I meant when did you paint this? I remember that you worked on wildlife drawings, then Eden's portrait for Adams. When I left Belle Terre, you were involved in a painting of Yancey. A surprise gift for his beach cottage. But I never had any idea you were doing this."

"I didn't paint this in the lowcountry, Marissa. Or even when I first came to the Rafter B. It was here at the Broken Spur in my evenings alone that I began to paint again."

"You did this from memory?"

"There were sketches." She would be surprised if she knew how often he'd drawn her through the years. He'd sketched her in the quiet times they were together. And later from memory. This work, which was to be an exorcism, he had painted from memory.

Proving he could never forget her.

"I didn't think anything could ever be as wonderful as the painting of Eden. But this…" Bowing her head, she fought for control. When she looked at him again, there was delight in her eyes. "I haven't the words to tell you."

"I don't want the words, sweetheart. But someday, I want the little girl we never had. One who will grow up to be as courageous as the lady in the portrait."

Marissa's face took on a warm glow. Her dark eyes were like black diamonds. And when Jefferson's someday came, she would tell him a child had been her third wish that day long ago in the swamp. Someday. But for now, they had this day. "It's over. Really over. We can have it all, love and a life together, without guilt, without fear."

The last of guilt and fear resolved, Jefferson caught her to him. "Starting now."

As he held her before the portrait, he knew Valentina was right, a chance remark or encounter could undermine the most carefully laid plans. But a chance remark and encounter could also put them aright again. "Thanks to Cristal."

Because she had reasons of her own to be thankful for both the wisdom and the example of so many wise women, Marissa agreed. "To Cristal, and all the women like her."

Marissa was working with the young mare that had officially become Bonita when the telephone in the tack room rang. Less than a week had passed since Menendez ceased to be a threat and she hadn't learned yet that all news needn't be bad news. Distracted from her routine, she glanced at Jefferson, who was putting away a mended bridle to answer the insistent summons.

She was dismounting when he reappeared. "Trouble?"

"I think maybe it's good news." Taking Bonita's reins and looping them over a rail, Jefferson wrapped his hand around Marissa's. "Let's give the horses a break and take a walk."

The grass was high and the stream full and glittering in the sun. It should have been a walk through a desert paradise, but Marissa was at the point of screaming when Jefferson stopped within the shade of a cottonwood and took her in his arms.

"That was Steve. They're coming home. Jakie's finished her courses early and wants to return to the ranch before school begins in Silverton."

"Will you go back to the Rafter B?" Marissa asked the first question that came to mind.

"Sandy's assured me there's a place there for me. Steve said the same thing." Jefferson's gaze strayed over the canyon and the ranch Steve Cody built. "But they've deliberately kept this as a small operation. I doubt they really want to change it."

"What will you do? Where will you go?"

"I'd like to go to Belle Terre. I've been thinking about it for days." Smiling down at her, he asked, "How would you like to be married in Eden's garden? And after that, look into pursuing your medical studies at the university? There's money I haven't touched, a gift from Adams. We could buy a horse farm. I could paint. The possibilities are endless."

There was nothing Marissa wanted more than to see Jefferson at peace with himself, and with his brothers. Nothing except Jefferson, himself. But was this right for him? "You can truly go home?"

"Yeah. I can go home now." Jefferson knew it was true. He could return to the land of his heart. For he'd learned a lot about loving, and sacrifice. About guilt and redemption.

Watching Marissa with Alejandro had taught him some sacrifices weren't truly sacrifices, but a deeper expression of love. Love that crippling guilt dishonored. "There are some things I need to say to Adams. Most of all, I need to tell him what loving you has taught me."

Looking up at him, Marissa saw that for the first time there were no haunted shadows darkening eyes as blue as a summer sky. In that moment, her happiness knew no limits, for she, too, had learned the difference between duty and honor and love.

The first had been her responsibility as a daughter. The

second, a promise kept. The last a gift surpassing all else. A gift shared and returned by Jefferson.

"Regrets, my love?" He questioned her thoughtfulness.

"I'll miss the canyon." Her gaze strayed over the familiar land. "And Juan and Marta, and Alejandro. But we can visit. So can they. Often. Or even come with us. But what about Satan?"

"My disobedient hound?" Jefferson lifted a teasing brow.

"Whose disobedience may have saved my life."

"He goes with us, everywhere. Always."

"Then how could I have regrets?" With smiling lips she kissed him. "Especially for loving you."

Her softly spoken words held the promise of a new life. From this day they would follow their hearts, together. And each day would be a celebration of a love that was the redemption of Jefferson Cade.

* * * * *

January 2002
THE REDEMPTION OF JEFFERSON CADE
#1411 by BJ James

Don't miss the fifth book in BJ James' exciting miniseries featuring irresistible heroes from Belle Terre, South Carolina.

M E N
of
Belle
Terre

February 2002
THE PLAYBOY SHEIKH
#1417 by Alexandra Sellers

Alexandra Sellers continues her sensual miniseries about powerful sheikhs and the women they're destined to love.

SONS
OF THE
DESERT

March 2002
BILLIONAIRE BACHELORS: STONE
#1423 by Anne Marie Winston

Bestselling author Anne Marie Winston's Billionaire Bachelors prove they're not immune to the power of love.

MAN OF THE MONTH

Some men are made for lovin'—and you're sure to love these three upcoming men of the month!

Available at your favorite retail outlet.

Silhouette®
Where love comes alive™

Visit Silhouette at www.eHarlequin.com   SDMOM02Q1

You are invited to enter the exclusive, masculine world of the...

Silhouette Desire's powerful miniseries features five wealthy Texas bachelors—all members of the state's most prestigious club— who set out to uncover a traitor in their midst... and discover their true loves!

THE MILLIONAIRE'S PREGNANT BRIDE
by Dixie Browning
February 2002 (SD #1420)

HER LONE STAR PROTECTOR
by Peggy Moreland
March 2002 (SD #1426)

TALL, DARK...AND FRAMED?
by Cathleen Galitz
April 2002 (SD #1433)

THE PLAYBOY MEETS HIS MATCH
by Sara Orwig
May 2002 (SD #1438)

THE BACHELOR TAKES A WIFE
by Jackie Merritt
June 2002 (SD #1444)

Available at your favorite retail outlet.

Where love comes alive™

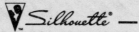

If you enjoyed what you just read,
then we've got an offer you can't resist!

Take 2 bestselling love stories FREE!

Plus get a FREE surprise gift!

Clip this page and mail it to Silhouette Reader Service™

IN U.S.A.	IN CANADA
3010 Walden Ave.	P.O. Box 609
P.O. Box 1867	Fort Erie, Ontario
Buffalo, N.Y. 14240-1867	L2A 5X3

YES! Please send me 2 free Silhouette Desire® novels and my free surprise gift. After receiving them, if I don't wish to receive anymore, I can return the shipping statement marked cancel. If I don't cancel, I will receive 6 brand-new novels every month, before they're available in stores! In the U.S.A., bill me at the bargain price of $3.34 plus 25¢ shipping and handling per book and applicable sales tax, if any*. In Canada, bill me at the bargain price of $3.74 plus 25¢ shipping and handling per book and applicable taxes**. That's the complete price and a savings of at least 10% off the cover prices—what a great deal! I understand that accepting the 2 free books and gift places me under no obligation ever to buy any books. I can always return a shipment and cancel at any time. Even if I never buy another book from Silhouette, the 2 free books and gift are mine to keep forever.

225 SEN DFNS
326 SEN DFNT

Name	(PLEASE PRINT)	
Address	Apt.#	
City	State/Prov.	Zip/Postal Code

* Terms and prices subject to change without notice. Sales tax applicable in N.Y.
** Canadian residents will be charged applicable provincial taxes and GST.
    All orders subject to approval. Offer limited to one per household and not valid to
    current Silhouette Desire® subscribers.
    ® are registered trademarks of Harlequin Enterprises Limited.

DES01   ©1998 Harlequin Enterprises Limited

Bestselling author
CAIT LONDON

**brings you another captivating book
in her unforgettable miniseries**

*One Western family finds the love that
legends—and little ones—are made of.*

**Available in February 2002:
TALLCHIEF: THE HUNTER**
Silhouette Desire #1419

Return to Tallchief Mountain as Adam Tallchief claims his
heritage and the woman he is destined to love. After twenty-
two years, Adam has come home to the family he didn't
know he has. But his old love and enemy, Jillian Green O'Malley,
is back, as well, and the passion that has always blazed
between them threatens to consume them both....

**"Cait London is an irresistible storyteller."
—*Romantic Times Magazine***

Available at your favorite retail outlet.

Where love comes alive™

Coming in January 2002 from Silhouette Books...

THE GREAT MONTANA COWBOY AUCTION

by

ANNE McALLISTER

With a neighbor's ranch at stake, Montana-cowboy-turned-Hollywood-heartthrob Sloan Gallagher agreed to take part in the Great Montana Cowboy Auction organized by Polly McMaster. Then, in order to avoid going home with an overly enthusiastic fan, he provided the money so that Polly could buy him and take him home for a weekend of playing house. But Polly had other ideas....

Also in the Code of the West

Available at your favorite retail outlet.

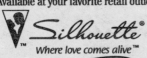

Where love comes alive™

Visit Silhouette at www.eHarlequin.com

PSGMCA

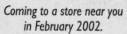

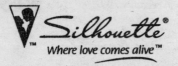